THE JOHN HARVARD LIBRARY

Bernard Bailyn
Editor-in-Chief

The John Harvard Library

The Gates Ajar

By

ELIZABETH STUART PHELPS

Edited by Helen Sootin Smith

THE BELKNAP PRESS OF
HARVARD UNIVERSITY PRESS
Cambridge, Massachusetts
1964

Distributed in Great Britain by Oxford University Press, London

Library of Congress Catalog Card Number 64–16068

Printed in the United States of America

Introduction

The Gates Ajar is a story placed in the last months of the Civil War, written as a series of entries in the diary of Mary Cabot, a twenty-four-year-old resident of the New England village of Homer. The first entries record Mary's grief for her brother Royal, to whom she was passionately devoted, and whose death in battle has just been reported. The condolences of acquaintances torment her; the rational pieties of the deacon of the Congregational Church infuriate her. Mary has lost faith in God's love and mercy. Her despair increases with each entry until a letter arrives announcing that her Aunt Winifred, whom she has never met, plans to come from Kansas to comfort her. Winifred, the widow of John Forceythe, arrives with her daughter Faith; and she leads Mary back to God. Conversations between the two women are recorded that reveal in some detail the prospect of a future reunion with Royal in a Kingdom of God very like Homer, Massachusetts. At the end of the book, Winifred dies, and Mary, now Faith's guardian, has found purpose in life as she awaits joys to come.

On the basis of this plot summary, one would hardly consider *The Gates Ajar* worth resurrecting. Indeed, even in its own day critics judged the book artistically trite and philo-

sophically unsound. But for three decades following its publication in 1868 it was enormously popular — popular to such
an extent and in such ways as to indicate that it answered a
crucial need of hundreds of thousands of readers.[1] In America
this need was no doubt related to the tensions created by
the Civil War; but the problems it dealt with transcended
politics and war. The book was addressed to the spiritual
disquiet created by the advance of science and the erosion of
traditional Christianity, which on a higher level produced
the doubts of such men as Tennyson, Arnold, and Hardy.
For its thousands of semieducated readers, an intellectual solu-
tion like transcendentalism or a rational system like Unitarian-
ism held little appeal. *The Gates Ajar*, in familiar but simple
and undemanding Christian terms, reassured those who had
come to doubt the immortality of the soul and who found
cold comfort in their ministers' vague assertions that life after
death was a reality. The book was a bridge between the high
citadel of Calvinist orthodoxy and the most inarticulate un-
certainties of popular faith; and while it was constructed of
materials that could not endure, for a time it enabled its audience to maintain a viable Christianity. Offering without dogma
a kind of personal immortality denied by science and Protestant orthodoxy alike, *The Gates Ajar* proved irresistible to
believers drawn to materialism, attractive to sentimentalists,
and comforting to the bereaved.

In artistic and philosophic terms, *The Gates Ajar* affords
a case study in the gradual assimilation of new forms. Behind
it lies an essentially Protestant and provincial culture; ahead
lies a secular, international world of letters. In origins it be-

[1] *The Gates Ajar* sold 80,000 copies in America and passed the 100,000
mark in England before the end of the century; it was translated into German, French, Dutch, Italian, and probably other languages. For thirty years
after its publication, letters reached the author from grateful readers, while
commercial exploitation of the book's popularity resulted in a "gates ajar"
collar and tippet, cigar, funeral wreath, and patent medicine, the last dis-
pensed with a free copy of the book.

longs to a New England genteel tradition that a democratic and materialistic society had largely outgrown. Elizabeth Stuart Phelps translates the old ideas into new terms using, without thought of formal purity, any literary form that will appeal to her audience. *The Gates Ajar* embodies sacred allegory, sentimental romance, Platonic dialogue, sermon, realistic story of New England life, and confessional diary. A similar absorption of diverse elements distinguishes the book's philosophic content, in which Calvinism joins romanticism, Scottish Common Sense philosophy, evolution, idealism, and materialism.

Neither intellectually nor artistically is *The Gates Ajar* an original book. Indeed, if it were original it would be surprising, since its author was a girl of twenty when she began, in 1864, to compose it. But as the granddaughter of one of Andover Theological Seminary's most illustrious teachers and the daughter of the man who would soon become its president, she inherited a unique position from which to transmit and adapt theological ideas. It is to Andover, consequently, and to its powerful seminary, that one must turn first to discover the origins of *The Gates Ajar* and to understand its importance in American cultural history.

I. THE ANDOVER BACKGROUND

Nowhere in America was orthodox Calvinism more rigorously and ostentatiously upheld than at Andover Seminary. Founded in 1808, three years after Harvard became Unitarian, by the supporters of the Old Calvinism and the New, or Hopkinsian, Divinity, it offered Calvinism on a nondenominational basis to candidates for the ministry. Its professors and Board of Visitors at regular intervals subscribed publicly to the Westminster Shorter Catechism and to the more severely Hopkinsian Andover Creed; and although this requirement was broadly interpreted, the principal doctrines of the catechism

and creed formed the basis of Andover teaching: the infalli-
bility of the Bible, the sovereignty of God, predestination,
total depravity, the limited atonement of Christ, and the con-
signment to hell of the nonelect. Andover theologians worked
to flesh this skeleton of dogma, but their endeavors, a century
after Jonathan Edwards, were poorly rewarded. In their popular appeal they continued to lose ground to the Unitarians on
the one hand and to the Methodists and Baptists on the other.

Yet even at Andover "pure" orthodox theology was in fact
an amalgam of various elements. Seventeenth-century Calvinism dominated the catechism, and eighteenth-century evan-
gelism the creed. From the eighteenth century also had come
enthusiasm and Scottish Common Sense philosophy. More
recently Kant and Hegel had taught Andover the distinction
between religious truth and the truth of empirical science. The
ideas of Friedrich Schleiermacher, with their romantic emphasis on the subjective experience of Christianity rather than
on doctrinal forms, had also penetrated Andover; and in the
1880's the institution, under a new faculty led by Egbert C.
Smyth, would demonstrate in the pages of the *Andover Re-
view* that it could adjust to the picture of the universe presented by Darwin.

The ideas of Elizabeth Stuart Phelps were simply those
available to her at Andover; but they were conveyed most
directly by two of the seminary's most distinguished teachers:
her maternal grandfather, Moses Stuart, and her tutor in
religion, Edwards A. Park. Stuart, who had come to Andover
in 1810 as Professor of Sacred Literature, introduced the study
of Hebrew in the seminary, and encouraged the study of German philosophy, philology, and Biblical higher criticism. Indeed, his enthusiasm for German thought led an investigating
committee to report that "the unrestrained cultivation of German Studies has evidently tended to chill the ardor of piety,
to impair belief in the fundamentals of revealed religion, and

even to induce, for the time, an approach to universal skepticism." [2] Far from fearing these studies, Stuart believed that if Andover were to become the "sacred West Point" he envisioned, its students would have to use modern weapons. In his *Letters* to William Ellery Channing (1819), Stuart defended the doctrine of the Trinity by suggesting that "logos becoming flesh" was the language of approximation.[3] In his teaching of this liberalism Stuart went unmolested, but the Andover Board of Visitors must have felt more at ease when Stuart's successor, Calvin Stowe, turned his 1852 inaugural address into a denunciation of German scholarship and philosophy in all its impious forms.

Elizabeth Stuart Phelps had few personal recollections of her grandfather, for he died in 1852 when she was eight years old. But Moses Stuart's influence was felt for a long time at the seminary, as well as in the home of his granddaughter. Elizabeth Stuart Phelps came to agree with Calvin Stowe that German scholarship and higher criticism were destroying faith; *The Gates Ajar* regards these pursuits as sinful temptations of the mind. On the other hand, she made the most of her freedom to read the Bible as poetic image, and somewhat incongruously classified both literal interpreters and higher critics as rigid dogmatists.

A more important Andover divine than Stuart during Elizabeth Stuart Phelps's formative years was Edwards A. Park, Professor of Theology from 1847 to 1881, who probably furnished his pupil with a prototype of the personally kind but theologically sterile minister who appears as Dr.

[2] Daniel Day Williams, *The Andover Liberals: A Study in American Theology* (New York, 1941), p. 17. Williams gives a full account of Andover's development. For the text of the seminary's statutes and laws, see Leonard Woods, *History of the Andover Theological Seminary* (Boston, 1884).

[3] Stuart's argument for understanding Biblical language as poetic image anticipates that of Horace Bushnell; he was probably influenced by the German theologian, Wilhelm M. L. De Wette.

Bland in *The Gates Ajar*. It was from him, she later wrote, that she had learned that "A sin is a wrong committed against God. God is an Infinite Being; therefore sin against Him is an infinite wrong. An infinite wrong against an Infinite Being deserves an infinite punishment." [4] When consulted years later, Park denied that he had ever taught this doctrine, and reminded her of the Andover position:

A sin once committed, always *deserves* punishment; and, as long as strict *Justice* is administered, the sin *must* be punished. Unless there be an Atonement, strict Justice *must* be administered; that is, Sin must be punished forever; but, on the ground of the Atonement, *Grace* may be administered instead of Justice, and then the sinner may be pardoned.[5]

His memory is probably correct, but to Elizabeth Stuart Phelps the difference between the two arguments was trifling compared with the similarity of their language and form.

Park's influence was actually more complex than this. For though he ended his career as a last-stand defender of orthodoxy, at mid-century he was a liberal influence within the seminary.[6] His most famous sermon, "The Theology of the Intellect and That of the Feelings," delivered in Boston in 1850 before a convention of Congregational ministers that included Trinitarians, Unitarians, Old and New Divinity Calvinists, was a conciliatory effort, marking Andover's first official departure from belief in the literal truth of Bible, catechism, and creed. In it Park distinguished between beliefs held rationally and those which commend themselves to the well-trained heart, arguing that it is the heart alone, synony-

[4] Elizabeth Stuart Phelps, *Chapters from a Life* (Boston, 1896), p. 70.
[5] *Chapters*, p. 71, note.
[6] Edwards Park, as well as Moses Stuart and Austin Phelps, adopted some of the ideas of Yale's Nathaniel W. Taylor, whose softened Calvinism questioned the doctrine of total depravity, and held men morally responsible only for acts freely performed. See Williams, *Andover Liberals*, p. 19.

mous to Park with the moral sense of humanity, that can pass
on the truth of doctrine, the Bible providing only an image
of truth that cannot be interpreted literally.

These ideas were commonplaces of the time, outside Andover, and it is probably an exaggeration to hold Park responsible for the alacrity with which Elizabeth Stuart Phelps
could dismiss dogma or Biblical evidence when it disagreed
with her most personal feelings.[7] Yet a passage like this, from
"The Theology of the Intellect and That of the Feelings,"
finds distinct echoes in *The Gates Ajar*:

Whenever we find, my brethren, that the words which we pro-
claim do not strike a responsive chord in the hearts of choice men
and women who look up to us for consolation, when they do not
stir our own souls, reach down to our hidden wants, and evoke sen-
sibilities which otherwise had lain buried under the cares of time;
or when they make an abiding impression that the divine government
is harsh, pitiless, insincere, oppressive, devoid of sympathy with our
most refined sentiments, reckless of even the most delicate emotion
of the tenderest nature, then we may infer that we have left out of
our theology some element which should have been inserted, or have
brought into it some element which we should have discarded. *Somewhere it must be wrong.*[8]

In the eyes of Elizabeth Stuart Phelps, Park's audience of
ministers did not sufficiently heed this warning; most of her
novels present Dr. Bland and his fellows as oblivious to the
"most refined sentiments" of the "tenderest nature." Their
doctrines cannot provide a person of complex and delicate
sensibility, especially a woman, with emotional comfort or
spiritual enlightenment.

[7] In 1848, two years earlier, Horace Bushnell had voiced similar beliefs
in his famous "Dogma and Spirit," an address delivered at Andover. But
Bushnell was an apostate, and Park a member of the orthodox establishment,
so not surprisingly the seminary listened more closely to Park.
[8] Quoted in Williams, *Andover Liberals*, p. 20. The text of this sermon
appears in Edwards A. Park, *Memorial Collection of Sermons* (Boston,
1902), pp. 75–123.

II. THE FAMILY ENVIRONMENT

An unusual family modified the intellectual influence of Andover on Elizabeth Stuart Phelps.[9] Her paternal grandfather, Eliakim Phelps, was a Congregational minister and revival preacher who, as a consequence of a peculiar series of events in one period in his life, left a strong imprint on his granddaughter's mind. For seven months, beginning in March 1850, his parsonage in Stratford, Connecticut, was overrun by poltergeists. Investigators confirmed the mysterious occurrences, and the case became famous as the first instance of "possession" in modern spiritualism.[10] Elizabeth Stuart Phelps, then a child of six, recalls in *Chapters from a Life* how the events retold over the years, affected her:

Night after night I have crept gasping to bed, and shivered for hours with my head under the clothes, after an evening spent in listening to this authentic and fantastic family tale. How the candlesticks walked out into the air from the mantelpiece and back again; how the chairs of skeptical visitors collected from all parts of the country to study what one had hardly then begun to call the "phenomena" at the parsonage at Stratford, Connecticut, hopped after the guests when they crossed the room; how the dishes at the table leaped, and the silver forks were bent by unseen hands, and cold turnips dropped from the solid ceiling; and ghastly images were found, composed of underclothing proved to have been locked at the time in drawers of which the only key lay all the while in Dr. Phelps's pocket; and how the mysterious agencies, purporting by alphabetical raps upon bedhead or on table to be in torments of the nether world, being asked what their host could do to relieve them, demanded a piece of squash pie.[11]

[9] The only full-length biography of the author, Mary Angela Bennett's *Elizabeth Stuart Phelps* (Philadelphia, 1939), provides a good deal of information about the Phelps and Stuart families.

[10] E. D. Branch, in *The Sentimental Years, 1836–1860* (New York, 1934), p. 371, gives a colorful but slightly inaccurate account of the events. See Joseph McCabe, *Spiritualism: A Popular History from 1847* (London, 1920), p. 44. Also see A. Conan Doyle, *The History of Spiritualism* (New York, 1926), I, 58.

[11] *Chapters*, pp. 6–7.

This account hardly does justice to the ingenuity of the Stratford poltergeist, who was almost certainly the younger son of Eliakim Phelps. This boy, about whom the family was understandably reticent, was sent off to school, where the accompanying spirits tore books and hid clothing, until they were finally expelled with him.

The almost mythic stories she heard in childhood about Eliakim Phelps's experience supplied imaginative themes for his granddaughter. Her early magazine stories recount instances of clairvoyance and other psychic phenomena, and *The Gates Ajar* and her two later novels about heaven theorize about the possibility of communication with the dead. Although she apparently had no personal experience with psychic phenomena, Elizabeth Stuart Phelps remained avidly interested in the research of the Psychical Society, hoping that its findings would prove the kind of immortality she hypothesizes in *The Gates Ajar*.[12]

Less obvious, but more pervasive in its influence upon her, was the discipline she received from her parents. Austin Phelps (1820–1890) was graduated from Andover Theological Seminary and ordained a Presbyterian minister in 1840. Two years later he married a daughter of Moses Stuart and assumed his duties as pastor of the Pine Street Church in Boston. There, in 1844, his first daughter was born and christened Mary Gray Phelps. Austin Phelps returned to Andover in 1848 as Professor of Sacred Rhetoric and Homiletics, a chair he held until his retirement in 1870. For the last ten years of his career, he also served as president of the seminary.

[12] Elizabeth Stuart Phelps's *The Struggle for Immortality* (Boston, 1889), contains several essays on psychic phenomena as potential proof of immortality. Boston in the 1880's became a spiritualist center, an event recorded by William Dean Howells in *The Undiscovered Country* (1880), and by Henry James in *The Bostonians* (1886). See Howard Mumford Jones, "Literature and Orthodoxy in Boston after the Civil War," *American Quarterly*, I (Summer, 1949), pp. 149–165.

Austin Phelps published a number of influential books, among them *The Still Hour* (1859), a very popular summary of sermons on prayer. He collaborated on the *Sabbath Hymn Book* (1859) and *Hymns and Choirs* (1860), the latter a practical guide for ministers in choosing hymns. In 1867, in *The New Birth*, Phelps described religious conversion as a gradual change of heart, an idea that occurs in *The Gates Ajar*, written at about the same time; and in retirement he summarized his rhetorical theory in two texts, *Theory of Preaching* (1881), and *English Style in Public Discourse* (1883), books which are particularly interesting historically for their early recognition of the evolutionary character of language.

Phelps's career was impressive, and though the daughter disagreed with much of the substance of his work, she retained always a grudging respect for ministerial professionalism. Yet the Austin Phelps who emerges from his daughter's 1891 memoir is a tormented figure, afflicted with inner demons far less playful than the poltergeists in his father's house. He suffered, she revealed, a morbid sense of guilt in early life; later he experienced several mental and physical breakdowns which at times brought his weak eyes near blindness; insomnia debilitated him for the last twenty years of his life. This was a pattern of illness, recognized now to have been a culturally sanctioned way of dealing with repression, which Elizabeth herself would repeat. It was not uncommon at the time; but the Phelps family, perhaps because of their strong Calvinistic sense of guilt, seemed to suffer more than their share of such ills. Elizabeth Stuart Phelps the elder (1815–1852) spent her short life in intermittent pain. Before her marriage to Austin Phelps she suffered repeated headaches, eye trouble, typhus fever, and what was vaguely identified as "cerebral disease." But she evidently suspected that an early acquaintance with the darker aspects of Calvinism might have unfortunate psychological effects, for she made an effort to give her children a cheerful faith. For her daughter, Mary Gray, and her first son, Moses Stuart, she wrote and illustrated Bible stories that were later published. Her *Sunny Side* (1851), a sentimental tale of life in the Pine Street parsonage, was a singular success; it sold 100,000 copies in a single year. But shortly thereafter, only a few months after her own father's death, Mrs. Phelps succumbed to a recurrence of "cerebral disease." Her bizarre funeral, at which, beside her coffin, her third child, Lawrence, was baptized, probably inspired a similar scene in *The Gates Ajar*.[13] Life and art so closely mirror one another in this case that it would be difficult to call either one the imitation.

Immediately after her mother's death, the eight-year-old Mary Gray assumed her mother's name. She did not welcome with enthusiasm either of the stepmothers her father provided. The first of these, her mother's sister, Mary Stuart, whom Austin Phelps married in 1854, died eighteen months later. Phelps's third wife, Mary Johnson, added two more sons to the household, giving Elizabeth Stuart Phelps four younger brothers in all.

These remarriages no doubt moved Phelps's daughter to the periphery of her father's life, with psychological consequences upon which the student of her writings is tempted if not obliged to speculate. How much of the passionate brother-sister relationship in *The Gates Ajar* can be accounted for by unconscious drives, and how much by the exaggeration of a literary convention by a fledgling writer? It is difficult to say, but the evidence suggests that her attachment to her father was intense, if not neurotic. The assumption of her mother's name and role as a writer may have served as one way of winning her father's affection; another was to become

---

[13] Austin Phelps gives an account of this scene in "Memorial of the Author," in Elizabeth Stuart Phelps, *The Last Leaf from Sunny Side* (Boston, 1860), p. 107.

as much like Austin Phelps as possible. Barred by her sex from his profession, Elizabeth Stuart Phelps became a lay preacher with an enormous congregation of readers. A strong feminist, she nonetheless experienced nearly all the real and neurotic ills to which her family was prone, including nervous illness, eye trouble, and for more than twenty years, insomnia. When she finally married, at the age of forty-four, she made an unconventional match with Herbert Dickenson Ward, a man of twenty-seven who depended on her for comfort through a long convalescence and, later, in all probability, for financial support as well.[14]

The case of Elizabeth Stuart Phelps raises in an interesting way the relation between personal psychology and literary expression. If, as seems likely, the incest theme of *The Gates Ajar* arose out of the author's unconscious mind, how then can we account for her overt recognition and calm dismissal of this charge when it reached her? She reports in *Chapters from a Life* on various misconceptions regarding the autobiographical character of *The Gates Ajar*, mentioning among other absurd charges that "I am haughtily taken to task by some unknown nature for allowing my heroine to be too much attached to her brother." [15] Could she have remained so unperturbed had the critic plucked the heart of her mystery? This seems an instance where unconscious psychological motivation operates within a conscious literary design. Her choice of the brother-sister motive probably appealed to her psychologically; at the same time, her conscious mind was fully satisfied by a literary explanation of her use of this theme.

[14] The marriage apparently did not bring great personal happiness. Ward, an 1888 graduate of Andover Seminary, soon began to spend less time with his wife, and more with younger friends. They collaborated on several historical novels of Biblical times. Usually Elizabeth Stuart Phelps wrote under her maiden name.

[15] *Chapters*, p. 124.

III. EDUCATION AND EARLY WRITINGS

Elizabeth Stuart Phelps's formal education recalls a nearly forgotten chapter of social history. She attended Abbot Academy, in Andover, then Mrs. Edwards' School for Young Ladies. Mrs. Edwards offered her students a curriculum equivalent to that of the men's colleges, with the exception of Greek and trigonometry. Elizabeth Stuart Phelps wrote of her training:

We studied what we called Mental Philosophy, to my unqualified delight; and Butler's *Analogy*, which I considered a luxury; and Shakespeare, whom I distantly but never intimately adored; Latin, to which dead language we gave seven years apiece out of our live girlhood; "Picciola" and "Undine," Racine, and Schiller, we dreamed over in the grove and the orchard; English literature is associated with the summer-house and the grape arbor, with flecks of shade and glints of light, and a sense of unmistakable privilege. There was physiology, which was scarcely work, and astronomy, which I found so exhilarating that I fell ill over it.[16]

Elizabeth Stuart Phelps, characteristically, shows less interest in the subjects themselves than in the private sentimental associations she formed with them. *The Gates Ajar* explains why Bishop Butler's *Analogy* was so luxurious: rejecting the logic of the syllogism as the conservative tool of dogmatic theology, she welcomed instinctively the logic of analogy as the living expression of nonlogical intuition, for which there were no accepted premises, and no tests for validity of conclusions except concurrence with the heart.

Her first story appeared in the *Youth's Companion* when she was only thirteen. Other juvenile fiction and Sunday school books followed, culminating in the popular "Gypsy" series of 1866–67, written at a time when she was devoting most of her energies to *The Gates Ajar*. From the start of

---

[16] *Chapters*, pp. 62–63.

her career she wrote secretly, showing her stories to no one, and composing them anywhere in the house where she could find silence and comfort, most frequently in bed and in the barn. Her attitude toward her writing was in the beginning antiprofessional, as befitted a cultivated young lady who did not need to earn her livelihood. She did not, she claims, until after *The Gates Ajar*, consider writing as a profession, and admits proudly in her autobiography that "It may be a humiliating fact, but it is the truth, that had my first story been refused, or even the second or the third, I should have written no more. For the opinion of important editors, and for the sacredness of market value in literary wares, as well as in professorships or cotton cloth, I had a kind of respect at which I sometimes wonder; for I do not recall that it was ever distinctly taught me. But, assuredly, if nobody had cared for my stories enough to print them, I should have been the last person to differ from the ruling opinion." And she offers would-be writers advice: "Do anything honest, but do not write, unless God calls you, and publishers want you, and people read you, and editors claim you. Respect the market laws. Lean on nobody." [17] She certainly did not debase her talent for the literary marketplace; her sensibility simply agreed with the taste of editors and readers. When publisher and public liked her work, she took it as a sign that God had called her to be a writer, and that she must therefore be a good writer, perhaps even an elect writer. One can well imagine how pleasant it must have been for Henry James, her literary acquaintance, when he talked shop with her. In 1908, William Dean Howells planned a composite novel by twelve popular authors, entitled *The Whole Family*. Henry James and Elizabeth Stuart Phelps wrote adjoining chapters, playing the parts of brother and sister. Thinly veiling his venom, James describes his "sister" as "deadly virtuous and

[17] This and the preceding quotation are from *Chapters*, pp. 77, 86.

deadly hard and deadly charmless — also, more than anything, deadly sure!" [18]

Elizabeth Stuart Phelps's first adult story appeared in *Harper's New Monthly Magazine* in January 1864. Two years earlier, a young Phillips Academy graduate, with whom she had been in love, Lieutenant Samuel Hopkins Thompson, was killed at Antietam. This event may have inspired "A Sacrifice Consumed," the story of an ugly seamstress whose loneliness is momentarily abated by a young man's love. When he is killed in the war, she finds the Christian fortitude to resign herself to her lonely existence. *Harper's* published seven more of her stories in the next two years, mainly on subjects that recur frequently in her later fiction: the consequences of intemperance, the fate of fallen women, and life after death.

The first of her stories to show concern for the social problems created by industrialism was "The Tenth of January," which appeared in the *Atlantic Monthly* in March 1868. The background of the story, based on the collapse in 1860 of the Pemberton Mill in nearby Lawrence, shows meticulous research. A structural defect caused the collapse, and a fire started accidentally by one of the rescuers killed eighty-eight of the workers trapped in the debris; they died, as she reports, singing hymns. These realistic details, however, remain in the background, as does the implicit condemnation of the company owners whose workers, mainly young girls, lived and worked under brutal conditions. The plot is conventionally sentimental, dealing with a love triangle fortuitously straightened by the tragedy.

Elizabeth Stuart Phelps all but witnessed the Pemberton Mill disaster, and had seen at first hand the living conditions

---

[18] *The Whole Family: A Novel by Twelve Authors* (New York, 1908), p. 154. Other contributors included Howells, Mary E. Wilkins Freeman, Mary Heaton Vorse, Mary Stewart Cutting, Elizabeth Jordan, John Kendrick Bangs, Edith Wyatt, Mary R. Shipman Andrews, Alice Brown, Henry van Dyke.

of laborers at Abbot Village, where she taught Sunday school in 1863. In these and other instances, personal acquaintance with a social evil prompted her fictional criticism. The two novels that followed *The Gates Ajar*, *Hedged In* (1870) and *The Silent Partner* (1871), deal with social and economic problems, a fact that has led Walter Fuller Taylor to regard Elizabeth Stuart Phelps as "the first American novelist to treat the social problems of the Machine Age seriously and at length." [19] But the realistic content of her fiction is usually reserved for background and minor characters; her plots are those of sentimental fiction. And unlike the Howells of *Hazard of New Fortunes* (1890) she does not try to comprehend the larger social or economic forces, nor does she question the essential, eternal rightness of the economic system. Finally, in contrast with later realist and naturalist writers, Elizabeth Stuart Phelps shows little real sympathy for the poor as a class, and scant understanding of the individual sufferer. She always sees society through the eyes of a well-born, conscientious Christian, who suffers from the unavoidable presence of evil, akin to ugliness, in her world. Horror at industrial abuses is subordinated to admiration for the fine women who undertake, single-handed, their correction.

IV. THE GATES AJAR

Like the novels and stories preceding and following it, *The Gates Ajar* embodies social criticism. Here Elizabeth Stuart Phelps's position is stronger, for she knew more about spiritual conditions than about the moral or physical conditions of industrial slums. No sudden glimpse of human misery prompted *The Gates Ajar*, but the author's long personal dissatisfaction with Andover's theology. In this anticlerical novel, the clergy serve as the equivalent of the company owners imagined in *The Silent Partner*: they are every bit as uncon-

---

[19] *The Economic Novel in America* (Chapel Hill, N.C., 1942), p. 58.

cerned with true human needs. Just as she found nothing
wrong with capitalism in theory, so she finds nothing essentially wrong with Christianity. Its failure lies in its clergy's
reluctance to adapt doctrine to the complex hearts of men
and women. Religion has the power to save men's souls, but
the conservative ministry, clinging to dogma, separate men
from God. In *The Gates Ajar*, as in her other stories, no mere
man can show the way; it requires a woman full of sensibility and free of dogma to recreate a God of love.

The heaven depicted by Winifred Forceythe for Mary
Cabot lies far from the abstract outline found in contemporary
sermons like Dr. Bland's. Dr. Bland's heaven is a dull place,
where people who on earth have subdued their natural affections meet in orderly formation, disembodied souls contem-
plating the infinite mind of an impersonal sovereign, and
occasionally sing hymns to the harper's tune. Finding absurd
this image of the City of God, Elizabeth Stuart Phelps predi-
cates a heavenly continuity with earth. Its landscape includes
the meadows, groves, and streams of Wordsworth's England,
as well as New England's cultivated gardens. Amid perfected
geological splendors, members of a free but organized society
live in private "mansions," read novels, attend concerts, even
marry and raise families. Here is a heaven where the crudest
or most refined tastes will be satisfied. Mechanics find machine
shops; scholars, libraries; tourists, side trips to the farther
nebulae. The Protestant idea of the dignity of labor so per-
vades *The Gates Ajar* that a man's occupation threatens to
become the measure of his dignity. In two later novels, Elizabeth Stuart Phelps fills in details of her vision, until heaven
becomes a utopian analogue of the world she knew, complete
with hospitals for sick souls who receive the ministrations of
spirit-doctors until they can assume full citizenship in the
City of God.[20]

[20] She elaborates this vision in *Beyond the Gates* (1883) and *The Gates*

The Gates Ajar portrays the spiritual world as a wish-ful-filling extension of the material world. Individualists are assured of continued personal identity in resurrected bodies that carefully preserve the essence of their earthly flesh. The promise of spiritual progress after death is held out, but the progress is strictly individual. Elizabeth Stuart Phelps invests heavenly society with a stability that perhaps only a Victorian could conceive.

The inhabitants of heaven maintain old ties and establish new ones with each other and with their families on earth. They see Jesus Christ, whose humanity makes Him one of them, and whose divinity sets Him apart. Hell exists in some undefined space, where it causes no discomfort to those in heaven. Its inhabitants are so few and so evil that those in heaven can politely ignore them. Election seems universal: any well-meaning person, however deficient his behavior, can expect to reach heaven. Missing is all sense of evil and of pre-destination; gone, too, is any emphasis on Christ's suffering for the sins of mankind. Men suffer enough for themselves in an imperfect world to deserve reunion with their loved ones in heaven. The territory beyond the gates seems to twentieth-century readers provincial in the extreme and so it seemed to Mark Twain, who called it "a mean little ten-cent heaven about the size of Rhode Island." [21] Still it was exactly the

Between (1887). The former describes the physical comforts and technological achievements of the heavenly city, and may have been read by Edward Bellamy. The latter, a better novel, concentrates on the psychological problems that face the skeptical narrator, Dr. Esmerald Thorne, when he arrives in heaven. A play, *Within the Gates* (1901), dramatizes *The Gates Between*. Less ambitious undertakings than *The Gates Ajar*, these later works take for granted the theology so laboriously unfolded in that book.

[21] *Mark Twain in Eruption*, ed. Bernard De Voto (New York, 1940), p. 247. Mark Twain's burlesque of *The Gates Ajar*, *Extract from Captain Stormfield's Visit to Heaven*, was unpublished until 1908 because of Mrs. Clemens' objections. He carries the premises of *The Gates Ajar* to their logical conclusion, and builds a heaven far more democratic and international, if less genteel, than that of Elizabeth Stuart Phelps. The American section of Captain Stormfield's heaven is peopled largely by Indians.

size of the world known to Elizabeth Stuart Phelps, and it appealed powerfully to hundreds of thousands of readers.[22]

How did a twenty-year-old girl conceive this heaven? Elizabeth Stuart Phelps offers two seemingly conflicting explanations for the composition of *The Gates Ajar*. She claims, like Mrs. Stowe, that "the angel said unto me 'Write!' and I wrote." [23] Elsewhere in her autobiography she admits that two or three years of solitary study went into its planning, and that she rewrote so many times that she knew the book by heart. Both stories may be true. We recognize her "angel" in the *Zeitgeist* of religious change, an angel who exacted from the earthling writer an arduous task of scholarship.

The Gates Ajar synthesizes all the philosophic and artistic patterns its young author could command. The authorities she cites include Plato, Augustine, Luther; contemporary ministers like the Reverend Andrew Kennedy Hutchinson Boyd and the Reverend Frederick William Robertson; lay preachers like "Gail Hamilton" (Mary Abigail Dodge), Dr. George Bush, and Isaac Taylor; popular religious thinkers like Bishop Butler and the Reverend Thomas Chalmers. To call her reading shallow is to mistake the nature of her selectivity. She had read carefully and refined her understanding in discussions with members of her family as well as others in the Andover community. The most prominent philosophic influence on

[22] Mark Twain was the last writer to take the book seriously enough for parody. Later critics have seen it as a curious landmark in the long decline of Puritanism. For modern views, see A. H. Quinn, *American Fiction: An Historical and Critical Survey* (New York, 1936), p. 195, and Van Wyck Brooks, *New England: Indian Summer, 1865–1915* (New York, 1940), pp. 79–82. The most interesting early criticism comes from Mrs. Margaret Oliphant, an author much admired by Elizabeth Stuart Phelps, and quoted frequently in *The Gates Ajar*. In an article on American books in *Blackwood's Magazine*, 110 (October 1871), 422–442, she passes over such American successes as *Little Women* and *Little Men* to praise *The Gates Ajar* and *The Luck of Roaring Camp* as the first worthy successors to the great works of Hawthorne and Mrs. Stowe.

[23] *Chapters*, p. 95.

The Gates Ajar seems to have been Butler's *Analogy of Religion, Natural and Revealed, to the Constitution and the Course of Nature* (1736), which offered Elizabeth Stuart Phelps an alternative to the syllogistic logic of Andover. Joseph Butler (1692–1752) had fought deism in his time with some of the same weapons Elizabeth Stuart Phelps uses to combat skepticism in her own. Assuming the existence of God, the known course of nature, and the limitations of human knowledge, Butler had argued inductively for the probability of life after death. His famous dictum, "probability is the very guide to life," came in his own work, as it surely does in *The Gates Ajar*, to mean "possibility," or even "certainty." Butler's emphasis on induction pleased the Scottish Common Sense philosophers, who extended his influence well into the nineteenth century. Indeed Butler's greatest popularity came after 1837 and lasted until Darwinism crushed teleological arguments from design.

However suggestive Butler's *Analogy* may have been, it did not satisfy all of Elizabeth Stuart Phelps's philosophic needs. Butler's universe remain the static, mechanical order of the eighteenth century, and he assumed that the supernatural world can best be apprehended by reason. As a rationalist, moreover, Butler opposed religious enthusiasm and evangelical Christianity. To confirm the final authority of her intuition of truth, Elizabeth Stuart Phelps turned to the German liberal theologians and philosophers, whose influence had long since reached Andover's faculty. Of these thinkers, the indirect influence of Schleiermacher on *The Gates Ajar* seems greatest, possibly because Coleridge expressed similar ideas in *Aids to Reflection*, a work well known in the seminary.

Liberal Christianity framed a dynamic and subjective religious faith by stressing the immanence of God, the humanity of Christ, and the perfectibility of man. Humanity afforded, through analogy, the best clue to the nature of God. Emphasis fell on man's natural goodness, not his fallen nature, and, by extension, on the possibility of securing his redemption through a humanitarian improvement of his earthly condition. Elizabeth Stuart Phelps responded to these currents of liberal theology, but added on the authority of Butler, Calvinism, and intuition, the one ingredient missing from most liberal theology: a concrete promise of personal immortality.

V. THE STRUCTURE OF THE GATES AJAR

The Gates Ajar, appealing nakedly to the wishful thinking of its readers, offered — in a predigested, synthesized, and sentimentalized form — the ideas of religious thinkers who on a higher plane were responding to the same philosophic currents as the audience. Yet, despite the apparently rambling, discursive character of the book, the deeper source of its power lies in its structure.

The Gates Ajar is a novel that mixes a variety of literary forms familiar to its author. The first of these is the sermon, a form in which Elizabeth Stuart Phelps had received almost professional training at Andover. Winifred serves as Mary's pastor, illustrating doctrine with Biblical quotations, snatches of familiar hymns, favorite lines from poems, allusions to current essays and novels. With the sermon, Elizabeth Stuart Phelps combines a second form: the realistic genre story of New England village life, so gracefully executed by Harriet Beecher Stowe and later local colorists.[24] Ladies in Homer participate in a pleasant, uneventful round of visits to friends, trips to town for butter or ribbon, evening chats over the register, Sunday church service, steaming chocolate for breakfast. Elizabeth Stuart Phelps evokes this innocent domestic life with some skill. The plot of *The Gates Ajar* comes from

[24] Perhaps her neighbor Mrs. Stowe's combination of village life and doctrinal criticism in *The Minister's Wooing* (1859) suggested this synthesis of forms, although her own mother's parsonage story, *The Sunny Side* (1851), offered a precedent even nearer home.

a third, related literary tradition — that of the sentimental novel. The domestic sentimental fiction written by and for women that dominated the literary market from about 1850 until the 1870's offered numerous prototypes of long-lost relatives, orphaned heroines, lingering and beautiful deaths, even the loss and regaining of faith. The device of casting the novel in diary form was common in sentimental fiction, but Elizabeth Stuart Phelps was probably inspired by a specific work, Eugénie de Guérin's *Journal*, published in 1862, in which the author continued after her brother's death to write "To Maurice in Heaven."

Allegory, the most important literary form used in *The Gates Ajar*, presents the modern reader with the greatest difficulties, although it is the form the author employs most rigorously.[25] Her precedents here were manifold. Allegory was so frequently used by her contemporaries that Mark Twain cautioned the readers of *Huckleberry Finn* (1885): "Persons attempting to find a motive in this narrative will be prosecuted; persons attempting to find a moral in it will be banished; persons attempting to find a plot in it will be shot."

This simple, sentimental tale presents problems that cannot be solved without moving to an allegorical level. How did Winifred hear of Roy's death? Is Mary's single-minded passion for her brother incestuous? What purpose does Winifred's death serve? In a modern novel, these and other logical gaps in the plot would constitute gross technical faults. Certainly, Mary's feeling for Roy would indicate the pathological state of either the character or the author. But some of the novel's

---

[25] Elizabeth Stuart Phelps wrote other allegorical stories, including her own favorite among her novels, *A Singular Life* (1895), which depicts the life of Bayard, a modern Christ. As a young minister, he rejects the hollow theology of Andover — which is realistically and amusingly described in the opening chapters — to go among the fishermen of Gloucester. There he fights drunkenness and prostitution, and succeeds admirably with the social gospel until his martyrdom.

defects of plot and characterization become understandable
when we realize that they are not accidents but signs pointing
to an allegorical reading.

The Gates Ajar, as a sacred allegory, relates the steps in
Christian redemption. The rude, willful behavior of Mary in
the opening chapters represents that of unregenerate man,
who has succumbed to the temptations of "the world, the
flesh, and the devil." [26] The temptation of the "world" traditionally figures as specious or false reasoning. Mary encounters
false persuasion in German poetry, and again in the loveless
metaphysics she hears in church. The "flesh," human weakness, is shown in Mary's inability to accept final physical
separation from Roy. The strength of this temptation leads
to such excesses as the following: "Roy, all I had in the wide
world, — Roy, with the flash in his eyes, with his smile that
lighted the house all up; with his pretty soft hair that I used
to curl and kiss about my finger, his bounding step, his strong
arms that folded me in and cared for me." The shock of his
loss brings Mary to the point of despair: the "devil" traditionally tempts by destroying faith with fear or violence.

Royal Cabot, however, did not die in vain. He is Christ,
dying in the Civil War for the sins of mankind. As Christ's
death redeemed mankind so that it could be reunited with
Him in heaven, so Roy's death saves Mary for everlasting life
with him. Christ sends his elect powers sufficient for their
salvation. These appear to Mary as heartfelt reason — which
explains Winifred's mysterious arrival — and Faith. Mary can
then renounce the deceits of the world, the flesh, and the devil,

[26] For the tripartite division of temptation and its use in the allegory of
Christian regeneration, see Elizabeth Marie Pope, "The Triple Equation,"
in *Paradise Regained: The Tradition and the Poem* (Baltimore, 1947), pp.
51–69. Nor was this an obscure tradition: the regeneration of fallen man
through Christ's redeeming sacrifice was central to Puritanism, and the
tripartite division of temptation is still repeated at christenings where the
Book of Common Prayer is used.

necessary steps in the drama of Christian regeneration. Winifred dies when reason has reached the limits of usefulness, so that Faith can fulfill the ritual of salvation.

Royal's Christlike qualities are everywhere stressed. In life he loved the little children; Mary pictures him crowned with "blood-red leaves," and "standing by the stainless cross." Other allegorical details seem nearly as obvious. Winifred's husband John worked among the heathen in the Kansas wilderness; his last act was the baptism of Faith. Winifred's name comes from Saint Boniface, the eighth-century English missionary who became the "Apostle of Germany." Like her namesake, Winifred has a special gift for converting those led astray by German thought.

One further allegorical principle probably patterned on the *Divine Comedy*, occurs in *The Gates Ajar* — the Platonic. Winifred like Diotima in the Platonic dialogue of their daily conversations leads Mary up the ladder of love. From the love of one fair form (Roy), Mary passes to the love of all fair forms (Winifred and Faith), thence to fair practices (Sunday school teaching), fair thoughts (heaven), and ultimately to a single thought of absolute beauty (Christ).

How much of this elaborate allegory did the average reader grasp? Few, probably, were aware of all the details. But most readers must have responded, consciously or unconsciously, to the power of the familiar allegory that lay in the public domain of all Christians. They need not have read Dante and Plato; the Bible and the Book of Common Prayer filled any gaps in their understanding of Mary's journey through the valley of the shadow of death, and her triumph over the world, the flesh, and the devil.

Each structural element in *The Gates Ajar* — sermon, diary, sentimental domestic plot, and allegory — follows a known literary convention. Elizabeth Stuart Phelps used the familiar to appeal to the common sense sentiments of ordinary men and women. The more familiar these sentiments, the more intuitive the response and, she believed, the greater the truths to which they led. *The Gates Ajar* elevated the sentiments of the common man by imbuing them with the philosophic meaning inherent in all deeply felt everyday experience. The allegory simply expressed philosophically what every reader felt or hoped.

VI. CHARACTERIZATION IN THE GATES AJAR

The characters in *The Gates Ajar* occupy positions on a chain of being descending from the most "ideal" to the most "real." Royal Cabot and John Forceythe, both spirits, are transcendent men, and they participate most fully in the Platonic form. Next comes Winifred, the ideal of humanity, mediating between the transcendent figures and Mary, the reality. Below Mary we find men and women deficient in humanity: Dr. Bland, Deacon Quirk, Mrs. Bland, Phoebe.

The most elevated characters are endowed first with a refined sensibility, and then with an equally fine adjustment of their feelings to God. Low birth will generally accompany a crude sensibility and a simple dogmatic faith; good birth assures a finely-tuned heart which, in turn, facilitates a free exploration of faith and aspiration toward God. Thus Roy, transcendent man and spontaneous child of nature, had little patience with church or dogma; yet he wrote Mary of the joy of his personal "friendship with Christ." The perfect natural man becomes the transcendent man, coming to Christ intuitively, like little Faith, without the artifice of theology. John Forceythe's faith cannot be entirely natural, like Roy's, since he is a trained minister. But John used his training to become the ideal minister, selecting his doctrines almost intuitively from the alternatives he learned and, more important, adjusting them to the needs of his parishioners. John's ultimate beliefs are precisely those passed on by Winifred to Mary.

These and other characters are defined by a carefully staged series of contrasts. Dr. Bland's conduct of a church service, for instance, compares unfavorably with that of John, who would never have chosen a hymn that was inappropriate to the weather. And as the two trained ministers form a contrast, so too do the lay preachers, Winifred and Deacon Quirk. Mary witnesses their confrontation:

I looked him over again, — hat, hoe, shirt, and all; scanned his obstinate old face with its stupid good eyes and animal mouth. Then I glanced at Winifred as she leaned forward in the afternoon light; the white, finely cut woman, with her serene smile and rapt, saintly eyes, — every inch of her, body and soul, refined not only by birth and training, but by the long nearness of her heart to Christ.

"Of the earth, earthy, Of the heavens, heavenly." The two faces sharpened themselves into two types. Which, indeed, was the better able to comprehend a "spiritooal heaven"?

These jibes at the man's speech and face are no mere snobbery. They indicate Deacon Quirk's incapacity for feeling, which depends largely on birth and breeding. Those dissatisfied with their earthly status may cultivate their hearts and minds in the hopes of occupying a higher position in heaven. But Quirk's bigotry and crudeness will probably unfit him to be more than a potato farmer in the next world, too.

Mary has the refined sensibility required for spiritual fulfillment, but initially she is spiritually blind. She has been confused by a theology that fits neither her sensitive soul nor God, and therefore believes herself a lost soul. She lacks the foresight and faith that Winifred supplies. We are left in no doubt about Mary's election when, consoling herself for the earthly years ahead, she writes, "Our hour is not yet

come. If the Master will that we should be about His Father's
business, what is that to us?"

VII. STYLE IN THE GATES AJAR

Elizabeth Stuart Phelps had learned rhetoric at Andover,
where the basic texts, which Austin Phelps later modified, were
written by the Scottish Common Sense rhetoricians, particularly Hugh Blair and Lord Kames. These works imparted to
their students a static principle of decorum. According to
them, nature has classified everything as high or low; all persons of taste agree on these classifications; correct literary
style conforms to nature's laws, and thus to man's intuitive
sense of beauty. *The Gates Ajar* maintains decorum with respect to the physical description of characters: Winifred's
eyes have "a curious, far-away look, and a steady lambent
light shines through them"; Deacon Quirk has "huge brown
elbows." But in an important way, Elizabeth Stuart Phelps
consciously and consistently breaches decorum. She takes an
iconoclastic delight in destroying remote images traditionally
associated with heaven, replacing them with ordinary images
intimately associated with the lives of her readers. She insists,
for example, that no matter how decorously harps fit heaven,
pianos belong there too. In this one respect she is part of the
tradition of the use of familiar language and imagery and the
rejection of poetic diction announced in Wordsworth's
Preface and carried much further in America by Mark Twain.
Basing her talk of heaven not, to be sure, on the thought and
language of the "common man" but on the thought and
language of the well-bred, modern woman, she boldly exchanged abstractions for concrete images that surprised almost
all of her readers, and outraged many.

Elizabeth Stuart Phelps needed a style that could senti-
mentalize and domesticate the metaphysical content of the
book, a style that would be conventional enough to win the

average woman's acceptance of unorthodox beliefs, yet shocking enough to strike emotional and intellectual sparks. The
diary provided an appropriately conventional frame for her
ideas. Decorum becomes irrelevant when a young girl ad-
dresses her private thoughts to a secret journal. Mary need
not dissemble strong emotion, nor avoid sudden and violent
shifts of feeling, nor keep high and low matter apart. Her
diary contains many "shocking" thoughts on man and God,
but the reader is continually made aware that Mary is a conventional girl who cannot help but voice, in the privacy of
her journal, her overpowering feelings. On one occasion, she
writes daringly: "Death and Heaven could not seem very
different to a Pagan from what they seem to me." But she
cushions this remark with the words: "I say this deliberately.
It has been deliberately forced upon me." The reader forgets
the blasphemy of what she says in the realization of how
strong her suffering must be to wring forth such a shocking
statement.

Within the domestic sentimental frame, Elizabeth Stuart
Phelps tried to propound difficult theological doctrines. The
resulting prose may seem stilted and unwieldy, but the prob-
lem of conveying such weighty matter by such a frail vehicle
was almost insuperable. Into the dainty mouths of two un-
intellectual ladies Elizabeth Stuart Phelps incongruously puts
great intellectual themes. Winifred, we learn, is a woman

who knows something about fate, free-will and foreknowledge absolute, who is not ignorant of politics, and talks intelligently of Agassiz's latest fossil, who can understand a German quotation, and has
heard of Strauss and Neander, who can dash her sprightliness ably
against [Dr. Bland's] old dry bones of metaphysics and theology, yet
never speak an accent above that essentially womanly voice of hers.

That "essentially womanly voice" continually jars us with
such patronizing conversational openings as, "You remember
Plato's old theory;" or such fashionably anti-intellectual statements as

No sooner do I find a pretty verse that is exactly what I want, than up hops a commentator, and says, this isn't according to text, and means something entirely different; and Barnes says this, and Stuart believes that, and Olshausen has demonstrated the other, and very ignorant it is in you, too, not to know it!

In this "reasoning" of Winifred with Mary, Elizabeth Stuart Phelps replays so many familiar tunes that the novel sounds like an echo of a Sunday church service followed by an afternoon at the parsonage. The allusiveness of *The Gates Ajar* seeks to persuade the heart of what the head is trying to follow in the Platonic dialogue. Among the reverberating "lost chords" we find the familiar hymn, "Jerusalem," Charles Lamb's "Dream Children," and Cowper's "God moves in a mysterious way." The book title comes from a hymn by Mrs. Adoniram Judson, containing the lines, "And when my angel guide went up,/He left the pearly gates ajar." The reader's sentimental associations with these and other works are expected to facilitate his acceptance of the less familiar but equally soul-stirring discursive argument.

The Gates Ajar opened for Elizabeth Stuart Phelps a forty-year literary career, in which she produced some fifty-seven books, as well as hundreds of stories, pamphlets, essays, and poems. She died on January 28, 1911, in her home in Newton Centre. At funeral services in the First Baptist Church, a Congregationalist minister presided, and the Lotus Club sang "Lead Kindly Light," "O Paradise," and "Beyond the Smiling and the Weeping." The death of the author of *The Gates Ajar*, three years before the outbreak of World War I, might be seen as the end of the dominance in popular literature of the small, feminine, New England sensibility.

HELEN SOOTIN SMITH

A NOTE ON THE TEXT

The Gates Ajar was published first in Boston by Fields, Osgood, and Company in November 1868, though the original title page bore the date 1869. The initial printing of four thousand copies sold out within a few weeks, and differed from the present and all subsequent texts only in that the dedication page carried the verb "nears" rather than "approaches." By 1884 Houghton Mifflin Company had published the fifty-fifth printing; the last printing was by the Regent Press in New York in 1910. For the present reprint the editor has taken no liberties with the original spelling and punctuation, but has added occasional numbered footnotes to identify the author's contemporary literary references.

THE GATES AJAR.

BY

ELIZABETH STUART PHELPS.

"Splendor! Immensity! Eternity! Grand words! Great things!
A little definite happiness would be more to the purpose."
MADAME DE GASPARIN.

BOSTON:
FIELDS, OSGOOD, & CO.,
SUCCESSORS TO TICKNOR AND FIELDS.
1 8 6 9.

[transcript of the title page of the second printing]

To my father, whose life, like a perfume from beyond the Gates, penetrates every life which approaches it, the readers of this little book will owe whatever pleasant thing they may find within its pages.

E. S. P.

ANDOVER, October 22, 1868.

I

ONE week; only one week to-day, this twenty-first of February.

I had been sitting here in the dark and thinking about it, till it seems so horribly long and so horribly short; it has been such a week to live through, and it is such a small part of the weeks that must be lived through, that I could think no longer, but lighted my lamp and opened my desk to find something to do.

I was tossing my paper about, — only my own: the packages in the yellow envelopes I have not been quite brave enough to open yet, — when I came across this poor little book in which I used to keep memoranda of the weather, and my lovers, when I was a school-girl. I turned the leaves, smiling to see how many blank pages were left, and took up my pen, and now I am not smiling any more.

If it had not come exactly as it did, it seems to me as if I could bear it better. They tell me that it should not have been such a shock. "Your brother had been in the army so long that you should have been prepared for anything. Everybody knows by what a hair a soldier's life is always hanging," and a great deal more that I am afraid I have not listened to. I suppose it is all true; but that never makes it any easier.

The house feels like a prison. I walk up and down and wonder that I ever called it home. Something is the matter with the sunsets; they come and go, and I do not notice them.

Something ails the voices of the children, snowballing down the street; all the music has gone out of them, and they hurt me like knives. The harmless, happy children! — and Roy loved the little children.

Why, it seems to me as if the world were spinning around in the light and wind and laughter, and God just stretched down His hand one morning and put it out.

It was such a dear, pleasant world to be put out!

It was never dearer or more pleasant than it was on that morning. I had not been as happy for weeks. I came up from the Post-Office singing to myself. His letter was so bright and full of mischief! I had not had one like it all the winter. I have laid it away by itself, filled with his jokes and pet names, "Mamie" or "Queen Mamie" every other line, and signed

"Until next time, your happy

"Roy."

I wonder if all brothers and sisters keep up the baby-names as we did. I wonder if I shall ever become used to living without them.

I read the letter over a great many times, and stopped to tell Mrs. Bland the news in it, and wondered what had kept it so long on the way, and wondered if it could be true that he would have a furlough in May. It seemed too good to be true. If I had been fourteen instead of twenty-four, I should have jumped up and down and clapped my hands there in the street. The sky was so bright that I could scarcely turn up my eyes to look at it. The sunshine was shivered into little lances all over the glaring white crust. There was a snowbird chirping and pecking on the maple-tree as I came in.

I went up and opened my window; sat down by it and drew a long breath, and began to count the days till May. I must have sat there as much as half an hour. I was so happy counting the days that I did not hear the front gate, and when I looked down a man stood there, — a great rough man, — who shouted up that he was in a hurry, and wanted seventy-five cents for a telegram that he had brought over from East Homer. I believe I went down and paid him, sent him away, came up here and locked the door before I read it.

Phoebe found me here at dinner time.

If I could have gone to him, could have busied myself with packing and journeying, could have been forced to think and plan, could have had the shadow of a hope of one more look, one word, I suppose I should have taken it differently. Those two words — "Shot dead" — shut me up and walled me in, as I think people must feel shut up and walled in, in Hell. I write the words most solemnly, for I know that there has been Hell in my heart.

It is all over now. He came back, and they brought him up the steps, and I listened to their feet, — so many feet; he used to come bounding in. They let me see him for a minute, and there was a funeral, and Mrs. Bland came over, and she and Phoebe attended to everything, I suppose. I did not notice nor think till we had left him out there in the cold and had come back. The windows of his room were opened, and the bitter wind swept in. The house was still and damp. Nobody was there to welcome me. Nobody would ever be * * * *

Poor old Phoebe! I had forgotten her. She was waiting at the kitchen window in her black bonnet; she took off my things and made me a cup of tea, and kept at work near me for a little while, wiping her eyes. She came in just now, when I had left my unfinished sentence to dry, sitting here with my face in my hands.

"Laws now, Miss Mary, my dear! This won't never do, — a rebellin' agin Providence, and singein' your hair on the lamp chimney this way! The dining-room fire's goin' beauti-ful, and the salmon is toasted to a brown. Put away them papers and come right along!"

II

February 23.

Who originated that most exquisite of inquisitions, the condolence system?

A solid blow has in itself the elements of its rebound; it arouses the antagonism of the life on which it falls; its relief is the relief of a combat.

But a hundred little needles pricking at us, — what is to be done with them? The hands hang down, the knees are feeble. We cannot so much as gasp, because they *are* little needles.

I know that there are those who like these calls; but why, in the name of all sweet pity, must we endure them without respect of persons, as we would endure a wedding reception or make a party-call?

Perhaps I write excitedly and hardly. I feel excited and hard.

I am sure I do not mean to be ungrateful for real sorrowful sympathy, however imperfectly it may be shown, or that near friends (if one has them) cannot give, in such a time as this, actual strength, even if they fail of comfort, by look and tone and love. But it is not near friends who are apt to wound, nor real sympathy which sharpens the worst of the needles. It is the fact that all your chance acquaintances feel called upon to bring their curious eyes and jarring words right into the silence of your first astonishment; taking you in a round of

morning calls with kid gloves and parasol, and the liberty to
turn your heart about and cut into it at pleasure. You may
quiver at every touch, but there is no escape, because it is
"the thing."

For instance: Meta Tripp came in this afternoon, — I have
refused myself to everybody but Mrs. Bland, before, but Meta
caught me in the parlor, and there was no escape. She had
come, it was plain enough, because she must, and she had come
early, because, she too having lost a brother in the war, she was
expected to be very sorry for me. Very likely she was, and
very likely she did the best she knew how, but she was — not
as uncomfortable as I, but as uncomfortable as she could be,
and was evidently glad when it was over. She observed, as she
went out, that I shouldn't feel so sad by and by. She felt very
sad at first when Jack died, but everybody got over that after
a time. The girls were going to sew for the Fair next week
at Mr. Quirk's, and she hoped I would exert myself and come.

Ah, well: —

> "First learn to love one living man,
>   Then mayst thou think upon the dead."

It is not that the child is to be blamed for not knowing
enough to stay away; but her coming here has made me wonder whether I am different from other women; why Roy was
so much more to me than many brothers are to many sisters.
I think it must be that there never *was* another like Roy. Then
we have lived together so long, we two alone, since father
died, that he had grown to me, heart of my heart, and life of
my life. It did not seem as if he *could* be taken, and I be left.

Besides, I suppose most young women of my age have their
dreams, and a future probable or possible, which makes the
very incompleteness of life sweet, because of the symmetry
which is waiting somewhere. But that was settled so long ago
for me that it makes it very different. Roy was all there was.

February 26.

Death and Heaven could not seem very different to a Pagan from what they seem to me.

I say this deliberately. It has been deliberately forced upon me. That of which I had a faint consciousness in the first shock takes shape now. I do not see how one with such thoughts in her heart as I have had can possibly be "regenerate," or stand any chance of ever becoming "one of the redeemed." And here I am, what I have been for six years, a member of an Evangelical church, in good and regular standing!

The bare, blank sense of physical repulsion from death, which was all the idea I had of anything when they first brought him home, has not gone yet. It is horrible. It was cruel. Roy, all I had in the wide world, — Roy, with the flash in his eyes, with his smile that lighted the house all up; with his pretty, soft hair that I used to kiss and curl about my fingers, his bounding step, his strong arms that folded me in and cared for me, — Roy snatched away in an instant by a dreadful God, and laid out there in the wet and snow, — in the hideous wet and snow, — never to kiss him, never to see him any more! * * * *

He was a good boy. Roy was a good boy. He must have gone to Heaven. But I know nothing about Heaven. It is very far off. In my best and happiest days, I never liked to think of it. If I were to go there, it could do me no good, for I should not see Roy. Or if by chance I should see him standing up among the grand, white angels, he would not be the old dear Roy. I should grow so tired of singing! Should long and fret for one little talk, — for I never said good by, and —

I will stop this.

A scrap from the German of Bürger, which I came across to-day, shall be copied here.

"Be calm, my child, forget thy woe,
And think of God and Heaven;
Christ thy Redeemer hath to thee
Himself for comfort given.

"O mother, mother, what is Heaven?
O mother, what is Hell?
To be with Wilhelm, — that's my Heaven?
Without him, — that's my Hell."

February 27.

Miss Meta Tripp, in the ignorance of her little silly heart, has done me a great mischief.

Phoebe prepared me for it, by observing, when she came up yesterday to dust my room, that "folks was all sayin' that Mary Cabot" — (Homer is not an aristocratic town, and Phoebe doffs and dons my title at her own sweet will) — "that Mary Cabot was dreadful low sence Royal died, and had n't ought to stay shut up by herself, day in and day out. It was behaving con-trary to the will of Providence, and very bad for her health, too." Moreover, Mrs. Bland, who called this morning with her three babies, — she never is able to stir out of the house without those children, poor thing! — lingered awkwardly on the door-steps as she went away, and hoped that Mary my dear would n't take it unkindly, but she did wish that I would exert myself more to see my friends and receive comfort in my affliction. She did n't want to interfere, or bother me, or — but — people would talk, and —

My good little minister's wife broke down all in a blush, at this point in her "porochial duties" (I more than suspect that her husband had a hand in the matter), so I took pity on her embarrassment, and said, smiling, that I would think about it.

I see just how the leaven has spread. Miss Meta, a little overwhelmed and a good deal mystified by her call here, pronounces "poor Mary Cabot *so* sad; she would n't talk about

Royal; and you could n't persuade her to come to the Fair; and she was so *sober!* — why, it was dreadful!"

Therefore, Homer has made up its mind that I shall become resigned in an arithmetical manner, and comforted according to the Rule of Three.

I wish I could go away! I wish I could go away and creep into the ground and die! If nobody need ever speak any more words to me! If anybody only knew *what* to say!

Little Mrs. Bland has ever been very kind, and I thank her with all my heart. But she does not know. She does not understand. Her happy heart is bound up in her little live children. She never laid anybody away under the snow without a chance to say good by.

As for the minister, he came, of course, as it was proper that he should, before the funeral, and once after. He is a very good man, but I am afraid of him, and I am glad that he has not come again.

Night.

I can only repeat and re-echo what I wrote this noon. If anybody knew *what* to say!

Just after supper I heard the door-bell, and, looking out of the window, I caught a glimpse of Deacon Quirk's old drab felt hat, on the upper step. My heart sank, but there was no help for me. I waited for Phoebe to bring up his name, desperately listening to her heavy steps, and letting her knock three times before I answered. I confess to having taken my hair down twice, washed my hands to a most unnecessary extent, and been a long time brushing my dress; also to forgetting my handkerchief, and having to go back for it after I was down stairs. Deacon Quirk looked tired of waiting. I hope he was.

O, what an ill-natured thing to say! What is coming over me? What would Roy think? What could he?

"Good evening, Mary," said the Deacon, severely, when I went in. Probably he did not mean to speak severely, but the truth is, I think he was a little vexed that I had kept him waiting. I said good evening, and apologized for my delay, and sat down as far from him as I conveniently could. There was an awful silence. "I came in this evening," said the Deacon, breaking it with a cough, "I came — hem! — to confer with you —"

I looked up. "I thought somebody had ought to come," continued the Deacon, "to confer with you as a Christian brother on your spiritooal condition."

I opened my eyes.

"To confer with you on your spiritooal condition," repeated my visitor. "I understand that you have had some unfortoonate exercises of mind under your affliction, and I observed that you absented yourself from the Communion Table last Sunday."

"I did."

"Intentionally?"

"Intentionally."

He seemed to expect me to say something more; and, seeing that there was no help for it, I answered.

"I did not feel fit to go. I should not have dared to go. God does not seem to me just now what He used to. He has dealt very bitterly with me. But, however wicked I may be, I will not mock Him. I think, Deacon Quirk, that I did right to stay away."

"Well," said the Deacon, twirling his hat with a puzzled look, "perhaps you did. But I don't see the excuse for any such feelings as would make it necessary. I think it my duty to tell you, Mary, that I am sorry to see you in such a rebellious state of mind."

I made no reply.

"Afflictions come from God," he observed, looking at me as

impressively as if he supposed that I had never heard the statement before. "Afflictions come from God, and, however
afflictin' or however crushin' they may be, it is our duty to
submit to them. Glory in triboolation, St. Paul says, glory in
triboolation." I continued silent.

"I sympathize with you in this sad dispensation," he proceeded. "Of course you was very fond of Royal; it's natural
you should be, quite natural —" He stopped, perplexed, I suppose, by something in my face. "Yes, it's very natural; poor
human nature sets a great deal by earthly props and affections.
But it's your duty, as a Christian and a church-member, to
be resigned."

I tapped the floor with my foot. I began to think that I
could not bear much more.

"To be resigned, my dear young friend. To say 'Abba,
Father,' and pray that the will of the Lord be done."

"Deacon Quirk!" said I, "I am *not* resigned. I pray the dear
Lord with all my heart to make me so, but I will not say that
I am, until I am, — if ever that time comes. As for those words
about the Lord's will, I would no more take them on my lips
than I would blasphemy, unless I could speak them honestly,
— and that I cannot do. We had better talk of something else
now, had we not?"

Deacon Quirk looked at me. It struck me that he would look
very much so at a Mormon or a Hottentot, and I wondered
whether he were going to excommunicate me on the spot.

As soon as he began to speak, however, I saw that he
was only bewildered, — honestly bewildered, and honestly
shocked: I do not doubt that I had said bewildering and shocking things.

"My friend," he said, solemnly, "I shall pray for you and
leave you in the hands of God. Your brother, whom He has
removed from this earthly life for His own wise —"

"We will not talk any more about Roy, if you please," I
interrupted; "*he* is happy and safe."

"Hem! — I hope so," he replied, moving uneasily in his chair; "I believe he never made a profession of religion, but there is no limit to the mercy of God. It is very unsafe for the young to think that they can rely on a death-bed repentance, but our God is a covenant-keeping God, and Royal's mother was a pious woman. If you cannot say with certainty that he is numbered among the redeemed, you are justified, perhaps, in hoping so."

I turned sharply on him, but words died on my lips. How could I tell the man of that short, dear letter that came to me in December, — that Roy's was no death-bed repentance, but the quiet, natural growth of a life that had always been the life of the pure in heart; of his manly beliefs and unselfish motives; of that dawning sense of friendship with Christ of which he used to speak so modestly, dreading lest he should not be honest with himself? "Perhaps I ought not to call myself a Christian," he wrote, — I learned the words by heart, — "and I shall make no profession to be such, till I am sure of it, but my life has not seemed to me for a long time to be my own. 'Bought with a price' just expresses it. I can point to no time at which I was conscious by any revolution of feeling of 'experiencing a change of heart,' but it seems to me that a man's heart might be changed for all that. I do not know that it is necessary for us to be able to watch every footprint of God. The *way* is all that concerns us, — to see that we follow it and Him. This I am sure of; and knocking about in this army life only convinces me of what I felt in a certain way before, — that it is the only way, and He the only guide *to* follow."

But how could I say anything of this to Deacon Quirk? — this my sealed and sacred treasure, of all that Roy left me the dearest. At any rate I did not. It seemed both obstinate and cruel in him to come there and say what he had been saying. He might have known that I would not say that Roy had gone to Heaven, if — why, if there had been the breath of a doubt. It is a possibility of which I cannot rationally conceive, but I suppose that his name would never have passed my lips.

So I turned away from Deacon Quirk, and shut my mouth, and waited for him to finish. Whether the idea began to struggle into his mind that he *might* not have been making a very comforting remark, I cannot say; but he started very soon to go.

"Supposing you are right, and Royal was saved at the eleventh hour," he said at parting, with one of his stolid efforts to be consolatory, that are worse than his rebukes, "if he is singing the song of Moses and the Lamb (he pointed with his big dingy thumb at the ceiling), *he* does n't rebel against the doings of Providence. All *his* affections are subdued to God, — merged, as you might say, — merged in worshipping before the great White Throne. He does n't think this miser'ble earthly spere of any importance, compared with that eternal and exceeding weight of glory. In the appropriate words of the poet, —

> 'O, not to one created thing
>   Shall our embrace be given,
> But all our joy shall be in God,
>   For only God is Heaven.'

Those are very spiritooal and scripteral lines, and it's very proper to reflect how true they are."

I saw him go out, and came up here and locked myself in, and have been walking round and round the room. I must have walked a good while, for I feel as weak as a baby.

Can the man in any state of existence be made to comprehend that he has been holding me on the rack this whole evening?

Yet he came under a strict sense of duty, and in the kindness of all the heart he has! I know, or I ought to know, that he is a good man, — far better in the sight of God to-night, I do not doubt, than I am.

But it hurts, — it cuts, — that thing which he said as he went out; because I suppose it must be true; because it seems to me greater than I can bear to have it true.

Roy, away in that dreadful Heaven, can have no thought of me, cannot remember how I loved him, how he left me all alone. The singing and the worshipping must take up all his time. God wants it all. He is a "Jealous God." I am nothing any more to Roy.

March 2.

And once I was much, — very much to him!

His Mamie, his poor Queen Mamie, — dearer, he used to say, than all the world to him, — I don't see how he can like it so well up there as to forget her. Though Roy was a very good boy. But this poor, wicked little Mamie, — why, I fall to pitying her as if she were some one else, and wish that some one would cry over her a little. I can't cry.

Roy used to say a thing, — I have not the words, but it was like this, — that one must be either very young or very ungenerous, if one could find time to pity one's self.

I have lain for two nights, with my eyes open all night long. I thought that perhaps I might see him. I have been praying for a touch, a sign, only for something to break the silence into which he has gone. But there is no answer, none. The light burns blue, and I see at last that it is morning, and go down stairs alone, and so the day begins.

Something of Mrs. Browning's has been keeping a dull, mechanical time in my brain all day.

"God keeps a niche
In Heaven to hold our idols: . . . . albeit
He brake them to our faces, and denied
That our close kisses should impair their white."

But why must He take them? And why should He keep them there? Shall we ever see them framed in their glorious

gloom? Will He let us touch them *then?* Or must we stand
like a poor worshipper at a Cathedral, looking up at his pictured saint afar off upon the other side?

Has everything stopped just here? Our talks together in the
twilight, our planning and hoping and dreaming together; our
walks and rides and laughing; our reading and singing and
loving, — these, then, are all gone out forever?

God forgive the words! but Heaven will never be Heaven
to me without them.

March 4.

Perhaps I had better not write any more here after this.

On looking over the leaves, I see that the little green book
has become an outlet for the shallower part of pain.

Meta Tripp and Deacon Quirk, gossip and sympathy that
have buzzed into my trouble and annoyed me like wasps (we
are apt to make more fuss over a wasp-sting than a sabre-cut),
just that proportion of suffering which alone can ever be put
into words, — the surface.

I begin to understand what I never understood till now, —
what people mean by the luxury of grief. No, I am sure that
I never understood it, because my pride suffered as much as
any part of me in that other time. I would no more have spent
two consecutive hours drifting at the mercy of my thoughts
than I would have put my hand into the furnace fire. The
right to mourn makes everything different. Then, as to
mother, I was very young when she died, and father, though I
loved him, was never to me what Roy has been.

This luxury of grief, like all luxuries, is pleasurable.
Though, as I was saying, it is only the shallow part of one's
heart — I imagine that the deepest hearts have their shallows —
which can be filled by it, still it brings a shallow relief.

Let it be confessed to this honest book, that, driven to it by
desperation, I found in it a wretched sort of content.

Being a little stronger now physically, I shall try to be a little braver; it will do no harm to try. So I seem to see that it was the content of poison, — salt-water poured between shipwrecked lips.

At any rate, I mean to put the book away and lock it up. Roy used to say that he did not believe in journals. I begin to see why.

·❦ III ❦·

I HAVE taken out my book, and am going to write again. But there is an excellent reason. I have something else than myself to write about.

This morning Phoebe persuaded me to walk down to the office, "To keep up my spirits and get some salt pork."

She brought my things and put them on me while I was hesitating; tied my victorine and buttoned my gloves; warmed my boots, and fussed about me as if I had been a baby. It did me good to be taken care of, and I thanked her softly; a little more softly than I am apt to speak to Phoebe.

"Bless your soul, my dear!" she said, winking briskly, "I don't want no thanks. It's thanks enough jest to see one of your old looks comin' over you for a spell, sence —"

She knocked over a chair with her broom, and left her sentence unfinished. Phoebe has always had a queer, clinging, superior sort of love for us both. She dandled us on her knees, and made all our rag-dolls, and carried us through measles and mumps and the rest. Then mother's early death threw all the care upon her. I believe that in her secret heart she considers me more her child than her mistress. It cost a great many battles to become established as "Miss Mary."

"I should like to know," she would say, throwing back her great square shoulders and towering up in front of me, — "I should like to know if you s'pose I'm a goin' to 'Miss' any-

body that I've trotted to Bamberry Cross as many times as I
have you, Mary Cabot! Catch me!"

I remember how she would insist on calling me "her baby"
after I was in long dresses, and that it mortified me cruelly
once when Meta Tripp was here to tea with some Boston
cousins. Poor, good Phoebe! Her rough love seems worth
more to me, now that it is all I have left me in the world. It
occurs to me that I may not have taken notice enough of her
lately. She has done her honest best to comfort me, and she
loved Roy, too.

But about the letter. I wrapped my face up closely in the
crêpe, so that, if I met Deacon Quirk, he should not recognize
me, and, thinking that the air was pleasant as I walked, came
home with the pork for Phoebe and a letter for myself. I did
not open it; in fact, I forgot all about it, till I had been at home
for half an hour. I cannot bear to open a letter since that
morning when the lances of light fell on the snow. They have
written to me from everywhere, — uncles and cousins and
old school-friends; well-meaning people; saying each the same
thing in the same way, — no, not that exactly, and very likely
I should feel hurt and lonely if they did not write; but sometimes I wish it did not all have to be read.

So I did not notice much about my letter this morning, till
presently it occurred to me that what must be done had better
be done quickly; so I drew up my chair to the desk, prepared
to read and answer on the spot. Something about the writing
and the signature rather pleased me: it was dated from Kansas,
and was signed with the name of my mother's youngest sister,
Winifred Forceythe. I will lay the letter in between these two
leaves, for it seems to suit the pleasant, spring-like day; besides,
I took out the green book again on account of it.

LAWRENCE, KANSAS, February 21.

MY DEAR CHILD, — I have been thinking how happy you
will be by and by because Roy is happy.

And yet I know — I understand —

You have been in all my thoughts, and they have been such pitiful, tender thoughts, that I cannot help letting you know that somebody is sorry for you. For the rest, the heart knoweth its own, and I am, after all, too much of a stranger to my sister's child to intermeddle.

So my letter dies upon my pen. You cannot bear words yet. How should I dare to fret you with them? I can only reach you by my silence, and leave you with the Heart that bled and broke for you and Roy.

Your Aunt,
WINIFRED FORCEYTHE.

POSTSCRIPT, February 23.

I open my letter to add, that I am thinking of coming to New England with Faith, — you know Faith and I have nobody but each other now. Indeed, I may be on my way by the time this reaches you. It is just possible that I may not come back to the West. I shall be for a time at your uncle Calvin's, and then my husband's friends think that they must have me. I should like to see you for a day or two, but if you do not care to see me, say so. If you let me come because you think you must, I shall find it out from your face in an hour. I should like to be something to you, or do something for you; but if I cannot, I would rather not come.

I like that letter.

I have written to her to come, and in such a way that I think she will understand me to mean what I say. I have not seen her since I was a child. I know that she was very much younger than my mother; that she spent her young ladyhood teaching at the South; — grandfather had enough with which to support her, but I have heard it said that she preferred to take care of herself; — that she finally married a poor minister, whose sermons people liked, but whose coat was shockingly shabby; that she left the comforts and elegances and friends of New England to go to the West and bury herself in an unheard-of little place with him (I think she must have loved him); that he afterwards settled in Lawrence; that there, after they had been married some childless years, this little Faith was born; and that there Uncle Forceythe died about three years ago; that is about all I know of her. I suppose her share of Grandfather Burleigh's little property supports her respectably. I understand that she has been living a sort of missionary life among her husband's people since his death, and that they think they shall never see her like again. It is they who keep her from coming home again, Uncle Calvin's wife told me once; they and one other thing, — her husband's grave.

I hope she will come to see me. I notice one strange thing about her letter. She does not use the ugly words "death" and "dying." I don't know exactly what she put in their places, but something that had a pleasant sound.

"To be happy because Roy is happy." I wonder if she really thinks it is possible.

I wonder what makes the words chase me about.

≼ IV ≽

May 5.

I AM afraid that my brave resolutions are all breaking down.

The stillness of the May days is creeping into everything; the days in which the furlough was to come; in which the bitter Peace has come instead, and in which he would have been at home, never to go away from me any more.

The lazy winds are choking me. Their faint sweetness makes me sick. The moist, rich loam is ploughed in the garden; the grass, more golden than green, springs in the warm hollow by the front gate; the great maple, just reaching up to tap at the window, blazes and bows under its weight of scarlet blossoms. I cannot bear their perfume; it comes up in great breaths, when the window is opened. I wish that little cricket, just waked from his winter's nap, would not sit there on the sill and chirp at me. I hate the bluebirds flashing in and out of the carmine cloud that the maple makes, and singing, singing, everywhere.

It is easy to understand how Bianca heard "The nightingales sing through her head," how she could call them "Owl-like birds," who sang "for spite," who sang "for hate," who sang "for doom."

Most of all I hate the maple. I wish winter were back again to fold it away in white, with its bare, black fingers only to come tapping at the window. "Roy's maple" we used to call it. How much fun he had out of that old tree!

As far back as I can remember, we never considered spring to be officially introduced till we had had a fight with the red blossoms. Roy used to pelt me well; but with that pretty chivalry of his, which was rare in such a little fellow, which developed afterwards into that rarer treatment of women, of which every one speaks who speaks of him, he would stop the play the instant it threatened roughness. I used to be glad, though, that I had strength and courage enough to make it some fun to him.

The maple is full of pictures of Roy. Roy, not yet over the dignity of his first boots, aiming for the cross-barred branch, coming to the ground with a terrible wrench on his ankle, straight up again before anybody could stop him, and sitting there on the ugly swaying bough as white as a sheet, to wave hi cap, — "There, I meant to do it, and I have!" Roy, chopping off the twigs for kindling-wood in his mud oven, and sending his hatchet right through the parlor window. Roy cutting leaves for me, and then pulling all my wreaths down over my nose every time I put them on! Roy making me jump half-way across the room with a sudden thump on my window, and looking out, I would see him with his hat off and hair blown from his forehead, framed in by the scented blossoms, or the quivering green, or the flame of blood-red leaves. But there is no end to them if I begin.

I had planned, if he came this week, to strip the richest branches, and fill his room.

May 6.

The May-day stillness, the lazy winds, the sweetness in the air, are all gone. A miserable northeasterly storm has set in. The garden loam is a mass of mud; the golden grass is drenched; the poor little cricket is drowned in a mud-puddle;

the bluebirds are huddled among the leaves, with their heads under their drabbled wings, and the maple blossoms, dull and shrunken, drip against the glass.

It begins to be evident that it will never do for me to live alone. Yet who is there in the wide world that I could bear to bring here — into Roy's place?

A little old-fashioned book, bound in green and gold, attracted my attention this morning while I was dusting the library. It proved to be my mother's copy of "Elia," — one that father had given her, I saw by the fly-leaf, in their early engagement days. It is some time since I read Charles Lamb; indeed, since the middle of February I have read nothing of any sort. Phoebe dries the Journal for me every night, and sometimes I glance at the Telegraphic Summary, and sometimes I don't.

"You used to be fond enough of books," Mrs. Bland says, looking puzzled, — regular blue-stocking, Mr. Bland called you (no personal objection to you, of course, my dear, but he *does n't* like literary women, which is a great comfort to me). Why don't you read and divert yourself now?"

But my brain, like the rest of me, seems to be crushed. I could not follow three pages of history with attention. Shakespeare, Wordsworth, Whittier, Mrs. Browning, are filled with Roy's marks, — and so down the shelf. Besides, poetry strikes as nothing else does, deep into the roots of things. One finds everywhere some strain at the fibres of one's heart. A mind must be healthily reconciled to actual life, before a poet — at least most poets — can help it. We must learn to bear and to work, before we can spare strength to dream.

To hymns and hymn-like poems, exception should be made. Some of them are like soft hands stealing into ours in the dark, and holding us fast without a spoken word. I do not know how many times Whittier's "Psalm," and that old cry of Cowper's, "God moves in a mysterious way," have quieted me, — just the sound of the words; when I was too wild to take in their meaning, and too wicked to believe them if I had.

As to novels, (by the way, Meta Tripp sent me over four yesterday afternoon, among which notice "Aurora Floyd" and "Uncle Silas,") the author of "Rutledge" expresses my feeling about them precisely.[1] I do not remember her exact words, but they are not unlike these. "She had far outlived the passion of ordinary novels; and the few which struck the depths of her experience gave her more pain than pleasure."

However, I took up poor "Elia" this morning, and stumbled upon "Dream Children," to which, for pathos and symmetry, I have read few things superior in the language. Years ago, I almost knew it by heart, but it has slipped out of memory with many other things of late. Any book, if it be one of those which Lamb calls "books which *are* books," put before us at different periods of life, will unfold to us new meanings, — wheels within wheels, delicate springs of purpose to which, at the last reading, we were stone-blind; gems which perhaps the author ignorantly cut and polished.

A sentence in this "Dream Children," which at eighteen I passed by with a compassionate sort of wonder, only thinking that it gave me "the blues" to read it, and that I was glad Roy was alive, I have seized upon and learned all over again now. I write it down to the dull music of the rain.

"And how when he died, though he had not been dead an hour, it seemed as if he had died a great while ago, such a distance there is betwixt life and death; and how I bore his death, as I thought, pretty well at first, but afterwards it haunted and haunted me; and though I did not cry or take it to heart as some do, and as I think he would have done if I had died, yet I missed him all day long, and knew not till then how much I

---

[1] *Uncle Silas* (1864) was a mystery novel by J. Sheridan Le Fanu; *Rutledge* (1860) was a novel published anonymously by Miriam Coles Harris; *Aurora Floyd* (1863), a novel by Mary Elizabeth Braddon.

had loved him. I missed his kindness and I missed his crossness, and wished him to be alive again to be quarrelling with him (for we quarrelled sometimes), rather than not have him again."

How still the house is! I can hear the coach rumbling away at the half-mile corner, coming up from the evening train. A little arrow of light has just cut the gray gloom of the West.

Ten o'clock.

The coach to which I sat listening rumbled up to the gate and stopped. Puzzled for the moment, and feeling as inhospitable as I knew how, I went down to the door. The driver was already on the steps, with a bundle in his arms that proved to be a rather minute child; and a lady, veiled, was just stepping from the carriage into the rain. Of course I came to my senses at that, and, calling to Phoebe that Mrs. Forceythe had come, sent her out an umbrella.

She surprised me by running lightly up the steps. I had imagined a somewhat advanced age and a sedate amount of infirmities, to be necessary concomitants of aunthood. She came in all sparkling with rain-drops, and, gently pushing aside the hand with which I was trying to pay her driver, said, laughing: —

"Here we are, bag and baggage, you see, 'big trunk, little trunk,' &c., &c. You did not expect me? Ah, my letter missed then. It is too bad to take you by storm in this way. Come, Faith! No, don't trouble about the trunks just now. Shall I go right in here?"

Her voice had a sparkle in it, like the drops on her veil, but it was low and very sweet. I took her in by the dining-room fire, and was turning to take off the little girl's things, when a soft hand stayed me, and I saw that she had drawn off the wet veil. A face somewhat pale looked down at me, — she is taller than I, — with large, compassionate eyes.

"I am too wet to kiss you, but I must have a look," she said, smiling. "That will do. You are like your mother, very like."

I don't know what possessed me, whether it was the sudden, sweet feeling of kinship with something alive, or whether it was her face or her voice, or all together, but I said: —

"I don't think you are too wet to be kissed," and threw my arms about her neck, — I am not of the kissing kind, either, and I had on my new bombazine, and she *was* very wet.

I thought she looked pleased.

Phoebe was sent to open the register in the blue room, and as soon as it was warm I went up with them, leading Faith by the hand. I am unused to children, and she kept stepping on my dress, and spinning around and tipping over, in the most astonishing manner. It strikingly reminded me of a top at the last gasp. Her mother observed that she was tired and sleepy. Phoebe was waiting around awkwardly up stairs, with fresh towels on her arm. Aunt Winifred turned and held out her hand.

"Well, Phoebe, I am glad to see you. This is Phoebe, I am sure? You have altered with everything else since I was here before. You keep bright and well, I hope, and take good care of Miss Mary?"

It was a simple enough thing, to be sure, her taking the trouble to notice the old servant, with whom she had scarcely ever exchanged a half-dozen words; but I liked it. I liked the way, too, in which it was done. It reminded me of Roy's fine, well-bred manner towards his inferiors, — always cordial, yet always appropriate; I have heard that our mother had much the same.

I tried to make things look as pleasant as I could down stairs, while they were making ready for tea. The grate was raked up a little, a bright supper-cloth laid on the table, and the curtains drawn. Phoebe mixed a hasty cake of some sort, and brought out the heavier pieces of silver, — teapot, &c.,

which I do not use when I am alone, because it is so much trouble to take care of them, and because I like the little Wedgwood set that Roy had for his chocolate.

"How pleasant!" said Aunt Winifred, as she sat down with Faith in a high chair beside her. Phoebe had a great hunt up garret for that chair; it has been stowed away there since it and I parted company. "How pleasant everything is here! I believe in bright dining-rooms. There is an indescribable dinginess to most that I have seen, which tends to anything but thankfulness. Homesick, Faith? No; that's right. I don't think we shall be homesick at Cousin Mary's."

If she had not said that, the probabilities are that they would have been, for I have fallen quite out of the way of active housekeeping, and have almost forgotten how to entertain a friend. But I do not want her good opinion wasted, and mean they shall have a good time if I can make it for them.

It was a little hard at first to see her opposite me at the table; it was Roy's place.

While she was sitting there in the light, with the dust and weariness of travel brushed away a little, I was able to make up my mind what this aunt of mine looks like.

She is young, then, to begin with, and I find it necessary to reiterate the fact, in order to get it into my stupid brain. The cape and spectacles, the little old woman's shawl and invalid's walk, for which I had prepared myself, persist in hovering before my bewildered eyes, ready to drop down on her at a moment's notice. Just thirty-five she is by her own showing; older than I, to be sure; but as we passed in front of the mirror together, once to-night, I could not see half that difference between us. The peace of her face and the pain of mine contrast sharply, and give me an old, worn look, beside her. After all, though, to one who had seen much of life, hers would be the true maturity perhaps, — the maturity of repose. A look in her eyes once or twice gave me the impression that she thinks me rather young, though she is far too wise and delicate to show it. I don't like to be treated like a girl. I mean to find out what she does think.

My eyes have been on her face the whole evening, and I believe it is the sweetest face — woman's face — that I have ever seen. Yet she is far from being a beautiful woman. It is difficult to say what makes the impression; scarcely any feature is accurate, yet the *tout ensemble* seems to have no fault. Her hair, which must have been bright bronze once, has grown gray — quite gray — before its time. I really do not know of what color her eyes are; blue, perhaps, most frequently, but they change with every word that she speaks; when quiet, they have a curious, far-away look, and a steady, lambent light shines through them. Her mouth is well cut and delicate, yet you do not so much notice that as its expression. It looks as if it held a happy secret, with which, however near one may come to her, one can never intermeddle. Yet there are lines about it and on her forehead, which are proof plain enough that she has not always floated on summer seas. She yet wears her widow's black, but relieves it pleasantly by white at the throat and wrists. Take her altogether, I like to look at her.

Faith is a round, rolling, rollicking little piece of mischief, with three years and a half of experience in this very happy world. She has black eyes and a pretty chin, funny little pink hands all covered with dimples, and a dimple in one cheek besides. She has tipped over two tumblers of water, scratched herself all over playing with the cat, and set her apron on fire already since she has been here. I stand in some awe of her; but after I have become initiated, I think we shall be very good friends. "Of all names in the catalogue," I said to her mother, when she came down into the parlor after putting her to bed, "Faith seems to be about the *most* inappropriate for this solid-bodied, twinkling little bairn of yours, with her pretty red cheeks, and such an appetite for supper!"

"Yes," she said, laughing, "there is nothing *spirituelle* about Faith. But she means just that to me. I could not call her anything else. Her father gave her the name." Her face changed, but did not sadden; a quietness crept into it and into her voice, but that was all.

"I will tell you about it some time, — perhaps," she added, rising and standing by the fire. "Faith looks like him." Her eyes assumed their distant look, "like the eyes of those who see the dead," and gazed away, — so far away, into the fire, that I felt that she would not be listening to anything that I might say, and therefore said nothing.

We spent the evening chatting cosily. After the fire had died down in the grate (I had Phoebe light a pine-knot there, because I noticed that Aunt Winifred fancied the blaze in the dining-room), we drew up our chairs into the corner by the register, and roasted away to our hearts' content. A very bad habit to sit over the register, and Aunt Winifred says she shall undertake to break me of it. We talked about everything under the sun, — uncles, aunts, cousins, Kansas and Connecticut, the surrenders and the assassination, books, pictures, music, and Faith, — O, and Phoebe and the cat. Aunt Winifred talks well, and does not gossip nor exhaust her resources; one feels always that she has material in reserve on any subject that is worth talking about.

For one thing I thank her with all my heart: she never spoke of Roy.

Upon reflection, I find that I have really passed a pleasant evening.

She knocked at my door just now, after I had written the last sentence, and had put away the book for the night. Thinking that it was Phoebe, I called, "Come in," and did not turn. She had come to the bureau, where I stood unbraiding my hair, and touched my arm, before I saw who it was. She had on a crimson dressing-gown of warm flannel, and her hair hung down on her shoulders. Although so gray, her hair is massive yet, and coils finely when she is dressed.

"I beg your pardon," she said, "but I thought you would not be in bed, and I came in to say, — let me sit somewhere else at the breakfast-table, if you like. I saw that I had taken 'the vacant place.' Good night, my dear."

It was such a little thing! I wonder how many people would have noticed it or taken the trouble to speak of it. The quick perception, the unusual delicacy, — these, too, are like Roy.

I almost wish that she had stayed a little longer. I almost think that I could bear to have her speak to me about him.

Faith, in the next room, seems to have wakened from a frightened dream, and I can hear their voices through the wall. Her mother is soothing and singing to her in the broken words of some old lullaby with which Phoebe used to sing Roy and me to sleep, years and years ago. The unfamiliar, home-like sound is pleasant in the silent house. Phoebe, on her way to bed, is stopping on the garret-stairs to listen to it. Even the cat comes mewing up to the door, and purring as I have not heard the creature purr since the old Sunday-night singing, hushed so long ago.

V

May 7.

I was awakened and nearly smothered this morning by a pillow thrown directly at my head.

Somewhat unaccustomed, in the respectable, old maid's life that I lead, to such a pleasant little method of salutation, I jerked myself upright, and stared. There stood Faith in her night-dress, laughing as if she would suffocate, and her mother, in search of her, was just knocking at the open door.

"She insisted on going to wake Cousin Mary, and would n't be washed till I let her; but I stipulated that she should kiss you softly on both your eyes."

"I did," said Faith, stoutly; "I kissed her eyes, both two of 'em, and her nose, and her mouth, and her neck; then I pulled her hair, and then I spinched her; but I thought she'd have to be banged a little. *Was n't* it a bang, though!"

It really did me good to begin the day with a hearty laugh. The days usually look so long and blank at the beginning, that I can hardly make up my mind to step out into them. Faith's pillow was the famous pebble in the pond, to which authors of original imagination invariably resort; I felt its little circles widening out all through the day. I wonder if Aunt Winifred thought of that. She thinks of many things.

For instance, afraid apparently that I should think I was

afflicted with one of those professional visitors who hold that a chance relationship justifies them in imposing on one from the beginning to the end of the chapter, she managed to make me understand, this morning, that she was expecting to go back to Uncle Forceythe's brother on Saturday. I was surprised at myself to find that this proposition struck me with dismay. I insisted with all my heart on keeping her for a week at the least, and sent forth a fiat that her trunks should be unpacked.

We have had a quiet, home-like day. Faith found her way to the orchard, and installed herself there for the day, overhauling the muddy grass with her bare hands to find dandelions. She came in at dinner-time as brown as a little nut, with her hat hanging down her neck, her apron torn, and just about as dirty as I should suppose it possible for a clean child to succeed in making herself. Her mother, however, seemed to be quite used to it, and the expedition with which she made her presentable I regard as a stroke of genius.

While Faith was disposed of, and the house still, Auntie and I took our knitting and spent a regular old woman's morning at the south window in the dining-room. In the afternoon Mrs. Bland came over, babies and all, and sent up her card to Mrs. Forceythe.

Supper-time came, and still there had not been a word of Roy. I began to wonder at, while I respected, this unusual silence.

While her mother was putting Faith to bed, I went into my room alone, for a few moments' quiet. An early dark had fallen, for it had clouded up just before sunset. The dull, gray sky and narrow horizon shut down and crowded in everything. A soldier from the village, who has just come home, was walking down the street with his wife and sister. The crickets were chirping in the meadows. The faint breath of the maple came up.

I sat down by the window, and hid my face in both my hands. I must have sat there some time, for I had quite forgotten that I had company to entertain, when the door softly opened and shut, and some one came and sat down on the couch beside me. I did not speak, for I could not, and, the first I knew, a gentle arm crept about me, and she had gathered me into her lap and laid my head on her shoulder, as she might have gathered Faith.

"There," she said, in her low, lulling voice, "now tell Auntie all about it."

I don't know what it was, whether the voice, or touch, or words, but it came so suddenly, — and nobody had held me for so long, — that everything seemed to break up and unlock in a minute, and I threw up my hands and cried. I don't know how long I cried.

She passed her hand softly to and fro across my hair, brushing it away from my temples, while they throbbed and burned; but she did not speak. By and by I sobbed out: —

"Auntie, Auntie, Auntie!" as Faith sobs out in the dark. It seemed to me that I must have help or die.

"Yes, dear. I understand. I know how hard it is. And you have been bearing it alone so long! I am going to help you, and you must tell me all you can."

The strong, decided words, "I am going to help you," gave me the first faint hope I have had, that I *could* be helped, and I could tell her — it was not sacrilege — the pent-up story of these weeks. All the time her hand went softly to and fro across my hair.

Presently, when I was weak and faint with the new comfort of my tears, "Aunt Winifred," I said, "I don't know what it means to be resigned; I don't know what it *means!*"

Still her hand passed softly to and fro across my hair.

"To have everything stop all at once! without giving me any time to learn to bear it. Why, you do not know, — it is just as if a great black gate had swung to and barred out the future, and barred out him, and left me all alone in any world that I can ever live in, forever and forever."

"My child," she said, with emphasis solemn and low upon the words, — "my child, I *do* know. I think you forget — my husband."

I had forgotten. How could I? We are most selfishly blinded by our own griefs. No other form than ours ever seems to walk with us in the furnace. Her few words made me feel, as I could not have felt if she had said more, that this woman who was going to help me had suffered too; had suffered perhaps more than I, — that, if I sat as a little child at her feet, she could teach me through the kinship of her pain.

"O my dear," she said, and held me close, "I have trodden every step of it before you, — every single step."

"But you never were so wicked about it! You never felt — why, I have been *afraid* I should hate God! You never were so wicked as that."

Low under her breath she answered "Yes," — this sweet, saintly woman who had come to me in the dark, as an angel might.

Then, turning suddenly, her voice trembled and broke: —

"Mary, Mary, do you think He *could* have lived those thirty-three years, and be cruel to you now? Think that over and over; only that. It may be the only thought you dare to have, — it was all I dared to have once, — but cling to it; *cling with both hands*, Mary, and keep it."

I only put both hands about her neck and clung there; but I hope — it seems, as if I clung a little to the thought besides; it was as new and sweet to me as if I had never heard of it in all my life; and it has not left me yet.

"And then, my dear," she said, when she had let me cry a little longer, "when you have once found out that Roy's God loves you more than Roy does, the rest comes more

easily. It will not be as long to wait as it seems now. It is n't
as if you never were going to see him again."

I looked up bewildered.

"What's the matter, dear?"

"Why, do you think I shall see him, — really see him?"

"Mary Cabot," she said abruptly, turning to look at me,
"who has been talking to you about this thing?"

"Deacon Quirk," I answered faintly, — "Deacon Quirk
and Dr. Bland."

She put her other arm around me with a quick movement,
as if she would shield me from Deacon Quirk and Dr. Bland.

"Do I think you will see him again? You might as well ask
me if I thought God made you and made Roy, and gave you
to each other. See him! Why, of course you will see him as
you saw him here."

"As I saw him here! Why, here I looked into his eyes, I
saw him smile, I touched him. Why, Aunt Winifred, Roy is
an angel!"

She patted my hand with a little, soft, comforting laugh.

"But he is not any the less Roy for that, — not any the less
your own real Roy, who will love you and wait for you and
be very glad to see you, as he used to love and wait and be
glad when you came home from a journey on a cold winter
night."

"And he met me at the door, and led me in where it was
light and warm!" I sobbed.

"So he will meet you at the door in this other home, and
lead you into the light and the warmth. And cannot that make
the cold and dark a little shorter? Think a minute!"

"But there is God, — I thought we went to Heaven to
worship Him, and — "

"Shall you worship more heartily or less, for having Roy
again? Did Mary love the Master more or less, after Lazarus
came back? Why, my child, where did you get your ideas

of God? Don't you suppose He *knows* how you love Roy?"

I drank in the blessed words without doubt or argument. I was too thirsty to doubt or argue. Some other time I may ask her how she knows this beautiful thing, but not now. All I can do now is to take it into my heart and hold it there.

Roy my own again, — not only to look at standing up among the singers, — but close to me; somehow or other to be as near as — to be nearer than — he was here, *really* mine again! I shall never let this go.

After we had talked awhile, and when it came time to say good night, I told her a little about my conversation with Deacon Quirk, and what I said to him about the Lord's will. I did not know but that she would blame me.

"Some time," she said, turning her great compassionate eyes on me, — I could feel them in the dark, — and smiling, "you will find out all at once, in a happy moment, that you can say those words with all your heart, and with all your soul, and with all your strength; it will come, even in this world, if you will only let it. But until it does, you do right, quite right, not to scorch your altar with a false burnt-offering. God is not a God to be mocked. He would rather have only the old cry: 'I believe; help mine unbelief,' and wait till you can say the rest. It has often grated on my ears," she added, "to hear people speak those words unworthily. They seem to me the most solemn words that the Bible contains, or that Christian experience can utter. As far as my observation goes, the good people — for they are good people — who use them when they ought to know better are of two sorts. They are people in actual agony, bewildered, racked with rebellious doubts, unaccustomed to own even to themselves the secret seethings of sin; really persuaded that because it is a Christian duty to have no will but the Lord's, they are under obligations to affirm that they have no will but the Lord's. Or else they are people who know no more about this pain of bereavement than a child. An affliction has passed over them, put them into mourning, made them feel uncomfortable till the funeral was over, or even caused them a shallow sort of grief, of which each week evaporates a little, till it is gone. These mourners air their trouble the longest, prate loudest about resignation, and have the most to say to you or me about our 'rebellious state of mind.' Poor things! One can hardly be vexed at them for pity. Think of being made so!"

"There is still another class of the cheerfully resigned," I suggested, "who are even more ready than these to tell you of your desperate wickedness — "

"People who have never had even the semblance of a trouble in all their lives," she interrupted. "Yes, I was going to speak of them. Of all miserable comforters, they are the most arrogant."

"As to real instant submission," she said presently, "there *is* some of it in the world. There are sweet, rare lives capable of great loves and great pains, which yet are kept so attuned to the life of Christ, that the cry in the Garden comes scarcely less honestly from their lips than from his. Such, like the St. John, are but one among the Twelve. Such, it will do you and me good, dear, at least to remember."

"Such," I thought when I was left alone, "you new dear friend of mine, who have come with such a blessed coming into my lonely days, — such you must be now, whatever you were once."

If I should tell her that, how she would open her soft eyes!

VI

As I was looking over the green book last night, Aunt Winifred came up behind me and softly laid a bunch of violets down between the leaves.

By an odd contrast, the contented, passionless things fell against those two verses that were copied from the German, and completely covered them from sight. I lifted the flowers, and held up the page for her to see.

As she read, her face altered strangely; her eyes dilated, her lip quivered, a flush shot over her cheeks and dyed her forehead up to the waves of her hair. I turned away quickly, feeling that I had committed a rudeness in watching her, and detecting in her, however involuntarily, some far, inner sympathy, or shadow of a long-past sympathy, with the desperate words.

"Mary," she said, laying down the book, "I believe Satan wrote that."

She laughed a little then, nervously, and paled back into her quiet, peaceful self.

"I mean that he inspired it. They are wicked words. You must not read them over. You will outgrow them some time with a beautiful growth of trust and love. Let them alone till that time comes. See, I will blot them out of sight for you with colors as blue as heaven, — the *real* heaven, where God *will* be loved the most."

She shook apart the thick, sweet nosegay, and, taking a half-dozen of the little blossoms, pinned them, dripping with fragrant dew, upon the lines. There I shall let them stay, and, since she wishes it, I shall not lift them to see the reckless words till I can do it safely.

This afternoon Aunt Winifred has been telling me about herself. Somewhat more, or of a different kind, I should imagine, from what she has told most people. She seems to love me a little, not in a proper kind of way, because I happen to be her niece, but for my own sake. It surprises me to find how pleased I am that she should.

That Kansas life must have been very hard to her, in contrast as it was with the smooth elegance of her girlhood; she was very young, too, when she undertook it. I said something of the sort to her.

"They have been the hardest and the easiest, the saddest and the happiest, years of all my life," she answered.

I pondered the words in my heart, while I listened to her story. She gave me vivid pictures of the long, bright bridal journey, overshadowed with a very mundane weariness of jolting coaches and railway accidents before its close; of the little neglected hamlet which waited for them, twenty miles from a post-office and thirty from a school-house; of the parsonage, a log-hut among log-huts, distinguished and adorned by a little lath and plastering, glass windows, and a door-step; — they drew in sight of it at the close of a tired day, with a red sunset lying low on the flats.

Uncle Forceythe wanted mission-work, and mission-work he found here with — I should say with a vengeance, if the expression were exactly suited to an elegantly constructed and reflective journal.

"My heart sank for a moment, I confess," she said, "but

it never would do, you know, to let him suspect that, so I smiled away as well as I knew how, shook hands with one or two women in red calico who had been "slickin' up inside," they said; went in by the fire, — it was really a pleasant fire, — and, as soon as they had left us alone, I climbed into John's lap, and, with both arms around his neck, told him that I knew we should be very happy. And I said — "

"Said what?"

She blushed a little, like a girl.

"I believe I said I should be happy in Patagonia — with him. I made him laugh at last, and say that my face and words were like a beautiful prophecy. And, Mary, if they were, it was beautifully fulfilled. In the roughest times, — times of ragged clothes and empty flour-barrels, of weakness and sickness and quack doctors, of cold and discouragement, of prairie fires and guerillas, — from trouble to trouble, from year's end to year's end, we were happy together, we two. As long as we could have each other, and as long as we could be about our Master's business, we felt as if we did not dare to ask for anything more, lest it should seem that we were ungrateful for such wealth of mercy."

It would take too long to write out here the half that she told me, though I wish I could, for it interested me more than any story that I have ever read.

After years of Christ-like toiling to help those rough old farmers and wicked bushwhackers to Heaven, the call to Lawrence came, and it seemed to Uncle Forceythe that he had better go. It was a pleasant, influential parish, and there, though not less hard at work, they found fewer rubs and more comforts; there Faith came, and there were their pleasant days, till the war. — I held my breath to hear her tell about Quantrill's raid. There, too, Uncle wasted through that death-in-life, consumption; there he "fell on sleep," she said, and there she buried him.

She gave me no further description of his death than those words, and she spoke them with her faraway, tearless eyes looking off through the window, and after she had spoken she was still for a time.

The heart knoweth its own bitterness; that grew distinct to me, as I sat, shut out by her silence. Yet there was nothing bitter about her face.

"Faith was six months old when we went," she said presently. "We had never named her: Baby was name enough at first for such a wee thing; then she was the only one, and had come so late that it seemed to mean more to us than to most to have a baby all to ourselves, and we liked the sound of the word. When it became quite certain that John must go, we used to talk it over, and he said that he would like to name her, but what, he did not tell me.

"At last, one night, after he had lain for a while thinking with closed eyes, he bade me bring the child to him. The sun was setting, I remember, and the moon was rising. He had had a hard day; the life was all scorched out of the air. I moved the bed up by the window, that he might have the breath of the rising wind. Baby was wide awake, cooing softly to herself in the cradle, her bits of damp curls clinging to her head, and her pink feet in her hands. I took her up and brought her just as she was, and knelt down by the bed. The street was still. We could hear the frogs chanting a mile away. He lifted her little hands upon his own, and said — no matter about the words — but he told me that as he left the child, so he left the name, in my sacred charge. — that he had chosen it for me, — that, when he was out of sight, it might help me to have it often on my lips.

"So there in the sunset and the moonrise, we two alone together, he baptized her, and we gave our little girl to God."

When she had said this, she rose and went over to the window, and stood with her face from me. By and by, "It was the fourteenth," she said, as if musing to herself, — "the four-teenth of June."

I remember now that Uncle Forceythe died on the four-teenth of June. It may have been that the words of that bap-tismal blessing were the last that they heard, either child or mother.

May 10.

It has been a pleasant day; the air shines like transparent gold; the wind sweeps like somebody's strong arms over the flowers, and gathers up a crowd of perfumes that wander up and down about one. The church-bells have rung out like silver all day. Those bells — especially the Second Advent at the farther end of the village — are positively ghastly when it rains.

Aunt Winifred was dressed bright and early for church. I, in morning dress and slippers, sighed and demurred.

"Auntie, *do* you expect to hear anything new?"

"Judging from your diagnosis of Dr. Bland, — no."

"To be edified, refreshed, strengthened, or instructed?"

"Perhaps not."

"Bored, then?"

"Not exactly."

"What do you expect?"

"There are the prayers and singing. Generally one can, if one tries, wring a little devotion from the worst of them. As to a minister, if he is good and commonplace, young and earn-est and ignorant, and I, whom he cannot help one step on the way to Heaven, consequently stay at home, Deacon Quirk, whom he might carry a mile or two, by and by stays at home also. If there is to be a 'building fitly joined together,' each stone must do its part of the upholding. I feel better to go half a day always. I never compel Faith to go, but I never have a chance, for she teases not to be left at home."

"I think it's splendid to go to church most the time," put in Faith, who was squatted on the carpet, counting sugared caraway seeds, — "all but the sermon. That is n't splendid. I don't like the gre-at big prayers 'n' things. I like caramary seeds, though; mother always gives 'em to me in meeting 'cause I'm a good girl. Don't you wish *you* were a good girl, Cousin Mary, so 's you could have some? Besides, I've got on my best hat and my button-boots. Besides, there used to be a real funny little boy up in meeting at home, and he gave me a little tin dorg once over the top the pew. Only mother made me give it back. O, you ought to seen the man that preached down at Uncle Calvin's! I tell you he was a bully old minister, — *he banged the Bible like everything!*"

"There's a devotional spirit for you!" I said to her mother.

"Well," she answered, laughing, "it is better than that she should be left to play dolls and eat preserves, and be punished for disobedience. Sunday would invariably become a guilty sort of holiday at that rate. Now, caraways or 'bully old ministers' notwithstanding, she carries to bed with her a dim notion that this has been holy time and pleasant time. Besides, the associations of a church-going childhood, if I can manage them genially, will be a help to her when she is older. Come, Faith! go and pull off Cousin Mary's slippers, and bring down her boots, and then she'll have to go to church. No, I *did n't* say that you might tickle her feet!"

Feeling the least bit sorry that I had set the example of a stay-at-home Christian before the child, I went directly up stairs to make ready, and we started after all in good season.

Dr. Bland was in the pulpit. I observed that he looked — as indeed did the congregation bodily — with some curiosity into our slip, where it has been a rare occurrence of late to find me, and where the light, falling through the little stained glass oriel, touched Aunt Winifred's thoughtful smile. I wonder whether Dr. Bland thought it was wicked for people to smile in church. No, of course he has too much sense. I wonder what it is about Dr. Bland that always suggests such questions.

It has been very warm all day, — that aggravating, unseasonable heat, which is apt to come in spasms in the early part of May, and which, in thick spring alpaca and heavy sack, one finds intolerable. The thermometer stood at 75° on the church-porch; every window was shut, and everybody's fan was fluttering. Now, with this sight before him, what should our observant minister do, but give out as his first hymn: "Thine earthly Sabbaths." "Thine earthly Sabbaths" would be a beautiful hymn, if it were not for those lines about the weather: —

> "No midnight shade, *no clouded sun,*
> *But sacred, high, eternal noon*"!

There was a great hot sunbeam striking directly on my black bonnet. My fan was broken. I gasped for air. The choir went over and over and *over* the words, spinning them into one of those indescribable tunes, in which everybody seems to be trying to get through first. I don't know what they called them, — they always remind me of a game of "Tag."

I looked at Aunt Winifred. She took it more coolly than I, but an amused little smile played over her face. She told me, after church, that she had repeatedly heard that hymn given out at noon of an intense July day. Her husband, she said, used to save it for the winter, or for cloudy afternoons. "Using means of grace," he called that.

However, Dr. Bland did better the second time, Aunt Winifred joined in the singing, and I enjoyed it, so I will not blame the poor man. I suppose he was so far lifted above this earth, that he would not have known whether he was preaching in Greenland's icy mountains, or on India's coral strand.

When he announced his text, "For our conversation is in

Heaven," Aunt Winifred and I exchanged glances of content. We had been talking about heaven on the way to church; at least, till Faith, not finding herself entertained, interrupted us by some severe speculations as to whether Maltese kitties were mulattoes, and "why the bell-ringer did n't jump off the steeple some night, and see if he could n't fly right up, the way Elijah did."

I listened to Dr. Bland as I have not listened for a long time. The subject was of all subjects nearest my heart. He is a scholarly man, in his way. He ought to know, I thought, more about it than Aunt Winifred. Perhaps he could help me.

His sermon, as nearly as I can recall it, was substantially this.

"The future life presented a vast theme to our speculation. Theories 'too numerous to mention' had been held concerning it. Pagans had believed in a coming state of rewards and punishments. What natural theology had dimly foreshadowed, Revelation had brought in, like a full-orbed day, with healing on its wings." I am not positive about the metaphors.

"As it was fitting that we should at times turn our thoughts upon the threatenings of Scripture, it was eminently suitable also that we should consider its promises.

"He proposed in this discourse to consider the promise of Heaven, the reward offered by Christ to his good and faithful servants.

"In the first place: What is heaven?"

I am not quite clear in my mind what it was, though I tried my best to find out. As nearly as I can recollect, however, —

"Heaven is an eternal state.

"Heaven is a state of holiness.

"Heaven is a state of happiness."

Having heard these observations before, I will not enlarge as he did upon them, but leave that for the "vivid imagination" of the green book.

"In the second place: What will be the employments of heaven?

"We shall study the character of God.

"An infinite mind must of necessity be eternally an object of study to a finite mind. The finite mind must of necessity find in such study supreme delight. All lesser joys and interests will pale. He felt at moments, in reflecting on this theme, that that good brother who, on being asked if he expected to see the dead wife of his youth in heaven, replied, 'I expect to be so overwhelmed by the glory of the presence of God, that it may be thousands of years before I shall think of my wife,' — he felt that perhaps this brother was near the truth."

Poor Mrs. Bland looked exceedingly uncomfortable.

"We shall also glorify God."

He enlarged upon this division, but I have forgotten exactly how. There was something about adoration, and the harpers harping with their harps, and the sea of glass, and crying, Worthy the Lamb! and a great deal more that bewildered and disheartened me so that I could scarcely listen to it. I do not doubt that we shall glorify God primarily and happily, but can we not do it in some other way than by harping and praying?

"We shall moreover love each other with a universal and unselfish love."

"That we shall recognize our friends in heaven, he was inclined to think, after mature deliberation, was probable. But there would be no special selfish affections there. In this world we have enmities and favoritisms. In the world of bliss our hearts would glow with holy love alike to all other holy hearts."

I wonder if he really thought *that* would make "a world of bliss." Aunt Winifred slipped her hand into mine under her cloak. Ah, Dr. Bland, if you had known how that little soft touch was preaching against you!

"In the words of an eminent divine, who has long since entered into the joys of which he spoke: 'Thus, whenever the mind roves through the immense region of heaven, it will find, among all its innumerable millions, not an enemy, not a stranger, not an indifferent heart, not a reserved bosom. Disguise here, and even concealment, will be unknown. The soul will have no interests to conceal, *no thoughts to disguise.* A window will be opened in every breast, and show to every eye the rich and beautiful furniture within!'

"Thirdly: How shall we fit for heaven?"

He mentioned several ways, among which, — "We should subdue our earthly affections to God.

"We must not love the creature as the Creator. My son, give *me* thy heart. When he removes our friends from the scenes of time (with a glance in my direction), we should resign ourselves to his will, remembering that the Lord gave and the Lord hath taken away in mercy; that He is all in all; that He will never leave us nor forsake us; that *He* can never change or die."

As if that made any difference with the fact, that his best treasures change or die!

"In conclusion, —

"We infer from our text that our hearts should not be set upon earthly happiness. (Enlarged.)

"That the subject of heaven should be often in our thoughts and on our lips." (Enlarged.)

Of course I have not done justice to the filling up of the sermon; to the illustrations, metaphors, proof-texts, learning, and eloquence, — for though Dr. Bland cannot seem to think outside of the old grooves, a little eloquence really flashes through the tameness of his style sometimes, and when he was talking about the harpers, etc., some of his words were well chosen. "To be drowned in light," I have somewhere read, "may be beautiful; it is still to be drowned." But I have given the skeleton of the discourse, and I have given the sum of the

impressions that it left on me, an attentive hearer. It is fortu-
nate that I did not hear it while I was alone; it would have
made me desperate. Going hungry, hopeless, blinded, I came
back empty, uncomforted, groping. I wanted something actual, something pleasant, about this place into which Roy
has gone. He gave me glittering generalities, cold commonplace, vagueness, unreality, a God and a future at which I
sat and shivered.

Dr. Bland is a good man. He had, I know, written that
sermon with prayer. I only wish that he could be made to *see*
how it glides over and sails spendidly away from wants like
mine.

But thanks be to God who has provided a voice to answer
me out of the deeps.

Auntie and I walked home without any remarks (we over-
heard Deacon Quirk observe to a neighbor: "That's what I
call a good gospel sermon, now!"), sent Faith away to Phoebe,
sat down in the parlor, and looked at each other.

"Well?" said I.

"I know it," said she.

Upon which we both began to laugh.

"But did he say the dreadful truth?"

"Not as I find it in my Bible."

"That it is probable, only *probable* that we shall recognize — "

"My child, do not be troubled about that. It is not probable, it is sure. If I could find no proof for it, I should none
the less believe it, as long as I believe in God. He gave you
Roy, and the capacity to love him. He has taught you to
sanctify that love through love to Him. Would it be *like*
Him to create such beautiful and unselfish loves, — most like
the love of heaven of any type we know, — just for our
threescore years and ten of earth? Would it be like Him to
suffer two souls to grow together here, so that the separation

of a day is pain, and then wrench them apart for all eternity?
It would be what Madame de Gasparin calls, 'fearful irony
on the part of God.' " [2]

"But there are lost loves. There are lost souls."

"How often would I have gathered you, and ye would
not! That is not his work. He would have saved both soul
and love. They had their own way. We were speaking of
His redeemed. The object of having this world at all, you
know, is to fit us for another. Of what use will it have been,
if on passing out of it we must throw by forever its gifts, its
lessons, its memories? God links things together better than
that. Be sure, as you are sure of Him, that we shall be *ourselves* in heaven. Would you be yourself not to recognize
Roy? — consequently not to love Roy, for to love and to be
separated is misery, and heaven is joy."

"I understand. But you said you had other proof."

"So I have; plenty of it. If 'many shall come from the East
and from the West, and shall sit down in the kingdom of
God with Abraham, Isaac, and Jacob,' will they not be likely
to know that they are with Abraham, Isaac, and Jacob? or
will they think it is Shadrach, Meshach, and Abednego?

"What is meant by such expressions as 'risen *together*,'
'sitting *together* at the right hand of God,' 'sitting *together*
in heavenly places'? If they mean anything, they mean recog-
nitions, friendships, enjoyments.

"Did not Peter and the others know Moses when they
saw him? — know Elias when they saw him? Yet these men
were dead hundreds of years before the favored fishermen
were born.

---

[2] Comtesse de Gasparin (1813–1894), writer of travels and religious
works. This and the title-page quotation come from "The Paradise We
Fear," in *The Near and the Heavenly Horizons* (1862). This essay expresses
thoughts on heaven very like those in *The Gates Ajar*. Mme. de Gasparin
writes, for instance, "Paradise . . . is my native country, not a foreign
land; it is the house of my father, not the temple of an abstract divinity.
I do not see an indistinguishable throng of phantoms; I meet brothers and
dear friends."

"How was it with those 'saints which slept and arose' when Christ hung dead there in the dark? Were they not seen of many?"

"But that was a miracle."

"They were risen dead, such as you and I shall be some day. The miracle consisted in their rising then and there. Moreover, did not the beggar recognize Abraham? and — Well, one might go through the Bible finding it full of this promise in hints or assertions, in parables or visions. We are 'heirs of God,' 'joint heirs with Christ'; having suffered with Him, we shall be 'glorified *together*.' Christ himself has said many sure things: 'I will come and receive you, that where I am, there ye may be.' 'I will that they be with me where I am.' Using, too, the very type of Godhead to signify the eternal nearness and eternal love of just such as you and Roy, as John and me, he prays: 'Holy Father, keep them whom Thou hast given me, that *they may be one as we are.*'

"There is one place, though, where I find what I like better than all the rest; you remember that old cry wrung from the lips of the stricken king, — 'I shall go to him; but he will not return to me.'"

"I never thought before how simple and direct it is, and that, too, in those old blinded days."

"The more I study the Bible," she said, "and I study not entirely in ignorance of the commentators and the mysteries, the more perplexed I am to imagine where the current ideas of our future come from. They certainly are not in this book of gracious promises. That heaven which we heard about to-day was Dr. Bland's, not God's. 'It's aye a wonderfu' thing to me, as poor Lauderdale said, 'the way some preachers take it upon themselves to explain matters to the Almighty!'"[3]

"But the harps and choirs, the throne, the white robes, are

[3] Lauderdale, quoted frequently in *The Gates Ajar*, is a character in Mrs. Margaret Oliphant's *Son of the Soil* (1866), a novel Elizabeth Stuart Phelps must have read as *The Gates Ajar* neared completion.

all in Revelation. Deacon Quirk would put his great brown finger on the verses, and hold you there triumphantly."

"Can't people tell picture from substance, a metaphor from its meaning? That book of Revelation is precisely what it professes to be, — a vision, a symbol. A symbol of something, to be sure, and rich with pleasant hopes, but still a symbol. Now, I really believe that a large proportion of Christian church-members, who have studied their Bible, attended Sabbath schools, listened to sermons all their lives, if you could fairly come at their most definite idea of the place where they expect to spend eternity, would own it to be the golden city, with pearl gates, and jewels in the wall. It never occurs to them, that, if one picture is literal, another must be. If we are to walk golden streets, how can we stand on a sea of glass? How can we 'sit on thrones'? How can untold millions of us 'lie in Abraham's bosom'?

"But why have given us empty symbols? Why not a little fact?"

"They are not *empty* symbols. And why God did not give us actual descriptions of actual heavenly life, I don't trouble myself to wonder. He certainly had his reasons, and that is enough for me. I find from these symbols, and from his voice in my own heart, many beautiful things, — I will tell you some more of them at another time, — and, for the rest, I am content to wait. He loves me, and he loves mine. As long as we love Him, He will never separate Himself from us, or us from each other. That, at least, is *sure*."

"If that is sure, the rest is of less importance; — yes. But Dr. Bland said an awful thing!"

"The quotation from a dead divine?"

"Yes. That there will be no separate interests, no thoughts to conceal."

"Poor good man! He has found out by this time that he should not have laid down nonsense like that, without quali-

fication or demur, before a Bible-reading hearer. It was simply *his* opinion, not David's, or Paul's, or John's, or Isaiah's.
He had a perfect right to put it in the form of a conjecture.
Nobody would forbid his conjecturing that the inhabitants
of heaven are all deaf and dumb, or wear green glasses, or
shave their heads, if he chose, provided he stated that it was
conjecture, not revelation."

"But where does the Bible say that we shall have power to
conceal our thoughts? — and I would rather be annihilated
than to spend eternity with heart laid bare, — the inner temple
thrown open to be trampled on by every passing stranger!"

"The Bible specifies very little about the minor arrangements of eternity in any way. But I doubt if, under any circumstances, it would have occurred to inspired men to inform us that our thoughts shall continue to be our own. The
fact is patent on the face of things. The dead minister's supposition would destroy individuality at one fell swoop. We
should be like a man walking down a room lined with mirrors, who sees himself reflected in all sizes, colors, shades, at
all angles and in all proportions, according to the capacity
of the mirror, till he seems no longer to belong to himself,
but to be cut up into ellipses and octagons and prisms. How
soon would he grow frantic in such companionship, and beg
for a corner where he might hide and hush himself in the dark?

"That we shall in a higher life be able to do what we cannot in this, — judge fairly of each other's *moral* worth, —
is undoubtedly true. Whatever the Judgment Day may mean,
that is the substance of it. But this promiscuous theory of
refraction; — never!

"Besides, wherever the Bible touches the subject, it premises
our individuality as a matter of course. What would be the
use of talking, if everybody knew the thoughts of everybody
else?"

"You don't suppose that people talk in heaven?"

"I don't suppose anything else. Are we to spend ages of joy, a company of mutes together? Why not talk?"

"I supposed we should sing, — but — "

"Why not talk as well as sing? Does not song involve the faculty of speech? — unless you would like to make canaries of us."

"Ye-es. Why, yes."

"There are the visitors at the beautiful Mount of Transfiguration again. Did not they *talk* with each other and with Christ? Did not John *talk* with the angel who 'shewed him those things'?"

"And you mean to say — "

"I mean to say that if there is such a thing as common sense, you will talk with Roy as you talked with him here, — only not as you talked with him here, because there will be no troubles nor sins, no anxieties nor cares, to talk about; no ugly shades of cross words or little quarrels to be made up; no fearful looking-for of separation."

I laid my head upon her shoulder, and could hardly speak for the comfort that she gave me.

"Yes, I believe we shall talk and laugh and joke and play — "

"Laugh and joke in heaven!"

"Why not?"

"But it seems so — so — why, so wicked and irreverent and all that, you know."

Just then Faith, who, mounted out on the kitchen table, was preaching at Phoebe in comical mimicry of Dr. Bland's choicest intonations, laughed out like the splash of a little wave.

The sound came in at the open door, and we stopped to listen till it had rippled away.

"There!" said her mother, "put that child, this very minute, with all her little sins forgiven, into one of our dear Lord's many mansions, and do you suppose that she would be any the

less holy or less reverent for a laugh like that? Is he going
to check all the sparkle and blossom of life when he takes us
to himself? I don't believe any such thing.

"There were both sense and Christianity in what somebody wrote on the death of a humorous poet: —

'Does nobody laugh there, where he has gone, —
This man of the smile and the jest?'

— provided there was any hope that the poor fellow *had*
gone to heaven; if not, it was bad philosophy and worse religion.

"Did not David dance before the Lord with all his might?
A Bible which is full of happy battle-cries: 'Rejoice in the
Lord! make a joyful noise unto him! Give thanks unto the
Lord, for his mercy endureth!' — a Bible which exhausts its
splendid wealth of rhetoric to make us understand that the
coming life is a life of *joy*, no more threatens to make nuns
than mutes of us. I expect that you will hear some of Roy's
very old jokes, see the sparkle in his eye, listen to his laughing
voice, lighten up the happy days as gleefully as you may
choose; and that — "

Faith appeared upon the scene just then, with the interesting
information that she had bitten her tongue; so we talked no
more.

How pleasant, — how pleasant this is! I never supposed before that God would let any one laugh in heaven.

I wonder if Roy has seen the President. Aunt Winifred says
she does not doubt it. She thinks that all the soldiers must
have crowded up to meet him, and "O," she says, "what a
sight to see!"

⊷ VII ⊶

May 12.

AUNT WINIFRED has said something about going, but I cannot yet bear to hear of such a thing. She is to stay awhile
longer.

16th.

We have been over to-night to the grave.

She proposed to go by herself, thinking, I saw, with the
delicacy with which she always thinks, that I would rather
not be there with another. Nor should I, nor could I, with
any other than this woman. It is strange. I wished to go there
with her. I had a vague, unreasoning feeling that she would
take away some of the bitterness of it, as she has taken the
bitterness of much else.

It is looking very pleasant there now. The turf has grown
fine and smooth. The low arbor-vitæ hedge and knots of
Norway spruce, that father planted long ago for mother,
drop cool, green shadows that stir with the wind. My English
ivy has crept about and about the cross. Roy used to say
that he should fancy a cross to mark the spot where he might
lie; I think he would like this pure, unveined marble. May-
flowers cover the grave now, and steal out among the clover-
leaves with a flush like sunrise. By and by there will be roses,
and in August, August's own white lilies.

We went silently over, and sat silently down on the grass, the field-path stretching away to the little church behind us, and beyond, in front, the slope, the flats, the river, the hills cut in purple distance melting far into the east. The air was thick with perfume. Golden bees hung giddily over the blush in the grass. In the low branches that swept the grave a little bird had built her nest.

Aunt Winifred did not speak to me for a time, nor watch my face. Presently she laid her hand upon my lap, and I put mine into it.

"It is very pleasant here," she said then, in her very pleasant voice.

"I meant that it should be," I answered, trying not to let her see my lips quiver. "At least it must not look neglected. I don't suppose it makes any difference to *him*."

"I do not feel sure of that."

"What do you mean?"

"I do not feel sure that anything he has left makes no 'difference' to him."

"But I don't understand. He is in heaven. He would be too happy to care for anything that is going on in this woful world."

"Perhaps that is so," she said, smiling a sweet contradiction to her words, "but I don't believe it."

"What do you believe?"

"Many things that I have to say to you, but you cannot bear them now."

"I have sometimes wondered, for I cannot help it," I said, "whether he is shut off from all knowledge of me for all these years till I can go to him. It will be a great while. It seems hard. Roy would want to know something, if it were only a little, about me."

"I believe that he wants to know, and that he knows, Mary; though, since the belief must rest on analogy and conjecture, you need not accept it as demonstrated mathematics," she answered, with another smile.

"Roy never forgot me here!" I said, not meaning to sob.

"That is just it. He was not constituted so that he, remaining himself, Roy, could forget you. If he goes out into this other life forgetting, he becomes another than himself. That is a far more unnatural way of creeping out of the difficulty than to assume that he loves and remembers. Why not assume that? In fact, why assume anything else? Neither reason, nor the Bible, nor common sense, forbids it. Instead of starting with it as an hypothesis to be proved if we can, I lay it down as one of those probabilities for which Butler would say, 'the presumption amounts nearly to certainty'; and if any one can disprove it, I will hear what he has to say. There!" she broke off, laughing softly, "that is a sufficient dose of metaphysics for such a simple thing. It seems to me to lie just here: Roy loved you. Our Father, for some tender, hidden reason, took him out of your sight for a while. Though changed much, he can have forgotten nothing. Being *only out of sight*, you remember, not lost, nor asleep, nor annihilated, he goes on loving. To love must mean to think of, to care for, to hope for, to pray for, not less out of a body than in it."

"But that must mean — why, that must mean — "

"That he is near you. I do not doubt it."

The sunshine quivered in among the ivy-leaves, and I turned to watch it, thinking.

"I do not doubt," she went on, speaking low, — "I cannot doubt that our absent dead are very present with us. He said, 'I am with you alway,' knowing the need we have of him even to the end of the world. He must understand the need we have of them. I cannot doubt it."

I watched her as she sat with her absent eyes turned eastward, and her peculiar look — I have never seen it on another face — as of one who holds a happy secret; and while I watched I wondered.

"There is a reason for it," she said, rousing as if from a pleasant dream, — "a good sensible reason, too, it strikes me, independent of Scriptural or other proof."

"What is that?"

"That God keeps us briskly at work in this world."

I did not understand.

"Altogether too briskly, considering that it is a preparative world, to intend to put us from it into an idle one. What more natural than that we shall spend our best energies as we spent them here, — in comforting, teaching, helping, saving people whose very souls we love better than our own? In fact, it would be very *un*natural if we did not."

"But I thought that God took care of us, and angels, like Gabriel and the rest, if I ever thought anything about it, which I am inclined to doubt."

" 'God works by the use of means,' as the preachers say. Why not use Roy as well as Gabriel? What archangel could understand and reach the peculiarities of your nature as he could? or, even if understanding, could so love and bear with you? What is to be done? Will they send Roy to the planet Jupiter to take care of somebody's else sister?" I laughed in spite of myself; nor did the laugh seem to jar upon the sacred stillness of the place. Her words were drawing away the bitterness, as the sun was blotting the dull, dead greens of the ivy into its glow of golden color.

"But the Bible, Aunt Winifred."

"The Bible does *not* say a great deal on this point," she said, "but it does not contradict me. In fact, it helps me; and, moreover, it would uphold me in black and white if it were n't for one little obstacle."

"And that?"

"That frowning 'original Greek,' which Gail Hamilton denounces with her righteous indignation.[4] No sooner do I find a pretty verse that is exactly what I want, than up hops a commentator, and says, this is n't according to text, and means something entirely different; and Barnes says this, and Stuart believes that, and Olshausen has demonstrated the other, and very ignorant it is in you, too, not to know it! [5] Here the other day I ferreted out a sentence in Revelation that seemed to prove beyond question that angels and redeemed men were the same; where the angel says to John, you know, 'Am I not of thy brethren the prophets?' I thought that I had discovered a delightful thing which all the Fathers of the church had overlooked, and went in great glee to your Uncle Calvin, to be told that something was the matter, — a noun left out, or some other unanswerable and unreasonable horror, I don't know what; and that it did n't mean that he was of thy brethren the prophets at all!

"You see, if it could be proved that the Christian dead become angels, we could have all that we need, direct from God, about — to use the beautiful old phrase — the communion of saints. From Genesis to Revelation the Bible is filled with angels who are at work on earth. They hold sweet converse with Abraham in his tent. They are intrusted to save the soul of Lot. An angel hears the wail of Hagar. The beautiful feet of an angel bring the good tidings to maiden Mary. An angel's noiseless step guides Peter through the barred and bolted gate. Angels rolled the stone from the buried Christ, and angels sat there in the solemn morning, — O Mary! if we could have seen them!

[4] "Gail Hamilton" was the pseudonym of Mary Abigail Dodge, editor of *Our Young Folks* (1865–1867), and friend and correspondent of Elizabeth Stuart Phelps.

[5] Albert Barnes, Moses Stuart, and Hermann Olshausen were all biblical exegetes, professors of theology. Barnes, a Philadelphia Presbyterian clergyman, was tried for heresy and acquitted. Stuart was the author's illustrious grandfather. Olshausen was a professor of theology at several German universities.

"Then there is that one question, direct, comprehensive, —
we should not need anything else, — 'Are they not all ministering spirits, sent forth to minister to the heirs of salvation?'

"But you see it never seems to have entered those commentators' heads that all these beautiful things refer to any
but a superior race of beings, like those from whose ranks
Lucifer fell."

"How stupid in them!"

"I take comfort in thinking so; but, to be serious, even
admitting that these passages refer to a superior race, must
there not be some similarity in the laws which govern existence
in the heavenly world? Since these gracious deeds are performed by what we are accustomed to call 'spiritual beings,'
why may they not as well be done by people from this world
as from anywhere else? Besides, there is another point, and a
reasonable one, to be made. The word angel in the original *
means, strictly, *a messenger*. It applies to any servant of God,
animate or inanimate. An east wind is as much an angel as
Michael. Again, the generic terms, 'spirits,' 'gods,' 'sons of
God,' are used interchangeably for saints and for angels. So,
you see, I fancy that I find a way for you and Roy and me
and all of us, straight into the shining ministry. Mary, Mary,
would n't you like to go this very afternoon?"

She lay back in the grass, with her face upturned to the
sky, and drew a long breath, wearily. I do not think she
meant me to hear it. I did not answer her, for it came over
me with such a hopeless thrill, how good it would be to be
taken to Roy, there by his beautiful grave, with the ivy and
the May-flowers and the sunlight and the clover-leaves round
about; and that it could not be, and how long it was to wait,
— it came over me so that I could not speak.

"There!" she said, suddenly rousing, "what a thoughtless,
wicked thing it was to say! And I meant to give you only the

* ἄγγελος.

good cheer of a cheery friend. No, I do not care to go this afternoon, nor any afternoon, till my Father is ready for me. Wherever he has most for me to do, there I wish, — yes, I think I *wish* to stay. He knows best."

After a pause, I asked again, "Why did He not tell us more about this thing, — about their presence with us? You see if I could *know* it!"

"The mystery of the Bible lies not so much in what it says, as in what it does not say," she replied. "But I suppose that we have been told all that we can comprehend in this world. Knowledge on one point might involve knowledge on another, like the links of a chain, till it stretched far beyond our capacity. At any rate, it is not for me to break the silence. That is God's affair. I can only accept the fact. Nevertheless, as Dr. Chalmers says: 'It were well for us all could we carefully draw the line between the secret things which belong to God and the things which are revealed and belong to us and to our children.' [6] Some one else, — Whately, I think, — I remember to have noticed as speaking about these very subjects to this effect, — that precisely because we know so little of them, it is the more important that we 'should endeavor so to dwell on them as to make the most of what little knowledge we have.' " [7]

"Aunt Winifred, you are such a comfort!"

"It needs our best faith," she said, "to bear this reticence of God. I cannot help thinking sometimes of a thing Lauderdale said, — I am always quoting him, — from 'Son of the Soil,' you remember: 'It's an awfu' marvel, beyond my reach, when a word of communication would make a' the differ-

[6] Thomas Chalmers (1780–1847), Scottish divine and mathematician known for his *Astronomical Discourses* and for his contribution to the *Bridgewater Treatises, On the Adaptation of External Nature to the Physical Condition of Man* (1833).

[7] Archbishop Richard Whately of Dublin (1787–1848), logician and rhetorician, wrote *Christian Evidences* (1837), the work to which the author refers.

ence, why it's no permitted, if it were but to keep a heart from breaking now and then.' Think of poor Eugénie de Guérin, trying to continue her little journal 'To Maurice in Heaven,' till the awful, answerless stillness shut up the book and laid aside the pen.[8]

"But then," she continued, "there is this to remember, — I may have borrowed the idea, or it may be my own, — that if we could speak to them, or they to us, there would be no death, for there would be no separation. The last, the surest, in some cases the only test of loyalty to God, would thus be taken away. Roman Catholic nature is human nature, when it comes upon its knees before a saint. Many lives — all such lives as yours and mine — would become — "

"Would become what?"

"One long defiance to the First Commandment."

I cannot become used to such words from such quiet lips. Yet they give me a curious sense of the trustworthiness of her peace. "Founded upon a rock," it seems to be. She has done what it takes a lifetime for some of us to do; what some of us go into eternity, leaving undone; what I am afraid I shall never do, — sounded her own nature. She knows the worst of herself, and faces it as fairly, I believe, as anybody can do in this world. As for the best of herself, she trusts that to Christ, and he knows it, and we. I hope she, in her sweet humbleness, will know it some day.

"I suppose, nevertheless," she said, "that Roy knows what you are doing and feeling as well as, perhaps better than, he knew it three months ago. So he can help you without harming you."

I asked her, turning suddenly, how that could be, and yet

[8] Eugénie de Guérin (1805–1848) was a religious mystic whose *Journals* were published posthumously in 1861, and translated into English in 1865. "To Maurice in Heaven," the continuation of her journal after her brother's death, no doubt appealed to Elizabeth Stuart Phelps who was, at the time, engaged in a similar literary endeavor.

heaven be heaven, — how he could see me suffer what I had suffered, could see me sometimes when I supposed none but God had seen me, — and sing on and be happy.

"You are not the first, Mary, and you will not be the last, to ask that question. I cannot answer it, and I never heard of any who could. I feel sure only of this, — that he would suffer far less to see you than to know nothing about you; and that God's power of inventing happiness is not to be blocked by an obstacle like this. Perhaps Roy sees the end from the beginning, and can bear the sight of pain for the peace that he watches coming to meet you. I do not know, — that does not perplex me now; it only makes me anxious for one thing."

"What is that?"

"That you and I shall not do anything to make them sorry."

"To make them sorry?"

"Roy would care. Roy would be disappointed to see you make life a hopeless thing for his sake, or to see you doubt his Saviour."

"Do you think *that?*"

"Some sort of mourning over sin enters that happy life. God himself 'was grieved' forty years long over his wandering people. Among the angels there has been 'silence,' whatever that mysterious pause may mean, just as there is joy over one sinner that repenteth; another of my proof-texts that, to show that they are allowed to keep us in sight."

"Then you think, you really think, that Roy remembers and loves and takes care of me; that he has been listening, perhaps, and is — why, you don't think he may be *here?*"

"Yes, I do. Here, close beside you all this time, trying to speak to you through the blessed sunshine and the flowers, trying to help you and sure to love you, — right here, dear. I do not believe God means to send him away from you, either."

My heart was too full to answer her. Seeing how it was,

she slipped away, and, strolling out of sight with her face to the eastern hills, left me alone.

And yet I did not seem alone. The low branches swept with a little soft sigh across the grave; the May-flowers wrapped me in with fragrance thick as incense; the tiny sparrow turned her soft eyes at me over the edge of the nest, and chirped contentedly; the "blessed sunshine" talked with me as it touched the edges of the ivy-leaves to fire.

I cannot write it even here, how these things stole into my heart and hushed me. If I had seen him standing by the stainless cross, it would not have frightened or surprised me. There — not dead or gone, but *there* — it helps me and makes me strong!

"Mamie! little Mamie!"

O Roy, I will try to bear it all if you will only stay!

❧ VIII ❧

May 20.

THE nearer the time has come for Aunt Winifred to go, the more it has seemed impossible to part with her. I have run away from the thought like a craven, till she made me face it this morning, by saying decidedly that she should go on the first of the week.

I dropped my sewing; the work-basket tipped over, and all my spools rolled away under the chairs. I had a little time to think while I was picking them up.

"There is the rest of my visit at Norwich to be made, you know," she said, "and while I am there I shall form some definite plans for the summer; I have hardly decided what, yet. I had better leave here by the seven o'clock train, if such an early start will not incommode you."

I wound up the last spool, and turned away to the window. There was a confused, dreary sky of scurrying clouds, and a cold wind was bruising the apple-buds. I hate a cold wind in May. It made me choke a little, thinking how I should sit and listen to it after she was gone, — of the old, blank, comfortless days that must come and go, — of what she had brought, and what she would take away. I was a bit faint, I think, for a minute. I had not really thought the prospect through, before.

"Mary," she said, "what's the matter. Come here."

I went over, and she drew me into her lap, and I put my arms about her neck.

"I can *not* bear it," said I, "and that is the matter."

She smiled, but her smile faded when she looked at me.

And then I told her, sobbing, how it was; that I could not go into my future alone, — I could not do it! that she did not know how weak I was, — and reckless, — and wicked; that she did not know what she had been to me. I begged her not to leave me. I begged her to stay and help me bear my life.

"My dear! you are as bad as Faith when I put her to bed alone."

"But," I said, "when Faith cries, you go to her, you know."

"Are you quite in earnest, Mary?" she asked, after a pause. "You don't know very much about me, after all, and there is the child. It is always an experiment, bringing two families into lifelong relations under one roof. If I could think it best, you might repent your bargain."

"*I* am not 'a family,'" I said, feebly trying to laugh. "Aunt Winifred, if you and Faith only *will* make this your home, I can never thank you, never. I shall be entertaining my good angels, and that is the whole of it."

"I have had some thought of not going back," she said at last, in a low, constrained voice, as if she were touching something that gave her great pain, "for Faith's sake. I should like to educate her in New England, if — I had intended if we stayed to rent or buy a little home of our own somewhere, but I had been putting off a decision. We are most weak and most selfish sometimes when we think ourselves strongest and noblest, Mary. I love my husband's people. I think they love me. I was almost happy with them. It seemed as if I were carrying on his work for him. That was so pleasant!" She put me down out of her arms and walked across the room.

"I will think the matter over," she said, by and by, in her natural tones, "and let you know tonight."

She went away up stairs then, and I did not see her again until to-night. I sent Faith up with her dinner and tea, judging that she would rather see the child than me. I observed, when the dishes came down, that she had touched nothing but a cup of coffee.

I began to understand, as I sat alone in the parlor through the afternoon, how much I had asked of her. In my selfish distress at losing her, I had not thought of that. Faces that her husband loved, meadows and hills and sunsets that he has watched, the home where his last step sounded and his last word was spoken, the grave where she has laid him, — this last more than all, — call after her, and cling to her with yearning closeness. To leave them, is to leave the last faint shadow of her beautiful past. It hurts, but she is too brave to cry out.

Tea was over, and Faith in bed, but still she did not come down. I was sitting by the window, watching a little crescent moon climb over the hills, and wondering whether I had better go up, when she came in and stood behind me, and said, attempting to laugh: —

"Very impolite in me to run off so, was n't it? Cowardly, too, I think. Well, Mary?"

"Well, Auntie?"

"Have you not repented your proposition yet?"

"You would excel as an inquisitor, Mrs. Forceythe!"

"Then it shall be as you say; as long as you want us you shall have us, — Faith and me."

I turned to thank her, but could not when I saw her face. It was very pale; there was something inexpressibly sad about her mouth, and her eyelids drooped heavily, like one weary from a great struggle.

Feeling for the moment guilty and ashamed before her, as if I had done her wrong, "It is going to be very hard for you," I said.

"Never mind about that," she answered, quickly. "We will not talk about that. I knew, though I did not *wish* to know, that it was best for Faith. Your hands about my neck have settled it. Where the work is, there the laborer must be. It is quite plain now. I have been talking it over with them all the afternoon; it seems to be what they want."

"With *them*"? I started at the words; who had been in her lonely chamber? Ah, it is simply real to her. Who, indeed, but her Saviour and her husband?

She did not seem inclined to talk, and stole away from me presently, and out of doors; she was wrapped in her blanket shawl, and had thrown a shimmering white hood over her gray hair. I wondered where she could be going, and sat still at the window watching her. She opened and shut the gate softly; and, turning her face towards the churchyard, walked up the street and out of my sight. She feels nearer to him in the resting-place of the dead. Her heart cries after the grave by which she will never sit and weep again; on which she will never plant the roses any more.

As I sat watching and thinking this, the faint light struck her slight figure and little shimmering hood again, and she walked down the street and in with steady step.

When she came up and stood beside me, smiling, with the light knitted thing thrown back on her shoulders, her face seemed to rise from it as from a snowy cloud; and for her look, — I wish Raphael could have had it for one of his rapt Madonnas.

"Now, Mary," she said, with the sparkle back again in her voice, "I am ready to be entertaining, and promise not to play the hermit again very soon. Shall I sit here on the sofa with you? Yes, my dear, I am happy, quite happy."

So then we took this new promise of home that has come to make my life, if not joyful, something less than desolate, and analyzed it in its practical bearings. What a pity that all pretty dreams have to be analyzed! I had some notion about throwing our little incomes into a joint family fund, but she put a veto to that; I suppose because mine is the larger. She prefers to take board for herself and Faith; but, if I know myself, she shall never be suffered to have the feeling of a boarder, and I will make her so much at home in my house that she shall not remember that it is not her own.

Her visit to Norwich she has decided to put off until the autumn, so that I shall have her to myself undisturbed all summer.

I have been looking at Roy's picture a long time, and wondering how he would like the new plan. I said something of the sort to her.

"Why put any 'would' in that sentence?" she said, smiling. "It belongs in the present tense."

"Then I am sure he likes it," I answered, — "he likes it," and I said the words over till I was ready to cry for rest in their sweet sound.

22d.

It is Roy's birthday. But I have not spoken of it. We used to make a great deal of these little festivals, — but it is of no use to write about that.

I am afraid I have been bearing it very badly all day. She noticed my face, but said nothing till to-night. Mrs. Bland was down stairs, and I had come away alone up here in the dark. I heard her asking for me, but would not go down. By and by Aunt Winifred knocked, and I let her in.

"Mrs. Bland cannot understand why you don't see her, Mary," she said, gently. "You know you have not thanked her for those English violets that she sent the other day. I only thought I would remind you; she might feel a little pained."

"I can't to-night, — not to-night, Aunt Winifred. You must excuse me to her somehow. I don't want to go down."

"Is it that you don't 'want to,' or *is* it that you can't?" she said, in that gentle, motherly way of hers, at which I can never take offence. "Mary, I wonder if Roy would not a little rather that you would go down?"

It might have been Roy himself who spoke.

I went down.

⟢ IX ⟣

June 1.

Aunt Winifred went to the office this morning, and met Dr. Bland, who walked home with her. He always likes to talk with her.

A woman who knows something about fate, free-will, and foreknowledge absolute, who is not ignorant of politics, and talks intelligently of Agassiz's latest fossil, who can understand a German quotation, and has heard of Strauss and Neander,[9] who can dash her sprightliness ably against his old dry bones of metaphysics and theology, yet never speak an accent above that essentially womanly voice of hers, is, I imagine, a phenomenon in his social experience.

I was sitting at the window when they came up and stopped at the gate. Dr. Bland lifted his hat to me in his grave way, talking the while; somewhat eagerly, too, I could see. Aunt Winifred answered him with a peculiar smile and a few low words that I could not hear.

"But, my dear madam," he said, "the glory of God, you see, the glory of God is the primary consideration."

"But the glory of God *involves* these lesser glories, as a sidereal system, though a splendid whole, exists by the multiplied differing of one star from another star. Ah, Dr. Bland,

---

[9] David Friedrich Strauss, author of the *Life of Jesus* (1835), sought proof of the mythical character of gospel history. Johann August Wilhelm Neander, a German Protestant church historian and theologian, wrote the *General History of the Christian Religion and Church* (1825–1852).

you make a grand abstraction out of it, but it makes me cold,"
— she shivered, half playfully, half involuntarily, — "it makes
me cold. I am very much alive and human; and Christ was
human God."

She came in smiling a little sadly, and stood by me, watching the minister walk over the hill.

"How much does that man love his wife and children?"
she asked abruptly.

"A good deal. Why?"

"I am afraid that he will lose one of them, then, before
many more years of his life are past."

"What! he has n't been telling you that they are consump-
tive or anything of the sort?"

"O dear me, no," with a merry laugh, which died quickly
away: "I was only thinking, — there is trouble in store for
him; some intense pain, — if he is capable of intense pain, —
which shall shake his cold, smooth theorizing to the foundation. He speaks a foreign tongue when he talks of bereavement, of death, of the future life. No argument could convince him of that, though, which is the worst of it."

"He must think you shockingly heterodox."

"I don't doubt it. We had a little talk this morning, and he
regarded me with an expression of mingled consternation and
perplexity that was curious. He is a very good man. He is not
a stupid man. I only wish that he would stop preaching and
teaching things that he knows nothing about.

"He is only drifting with the tide, though," she added, "in
his views of this matter. In our recoil from the materialism of
the Romish Church, we have, it seems to me, nearly stranded
ourselves on the opposite shore. Just as, in a rebound from the
spirit which would put our Saviour on a level with Buddha or
Mahomet, we have been in danger of forgetting 'to begin as
the Bible begins,' with his humanity. It is the grandeur of in-
spiration, that it knows how to *balance* truth."

It had been in my mind for several days to ask Aunt Winifred something, and, feeling in the mood, I made her take off her things and devote herself to me. My question concerned what we call the "intermediate state."

"I have been expecting that," she said; "what about it?"

"What *is* it?"

"Life and activity."

"We do not go to sleep, of course."

"I believe that notion is about exploded, though clear thinkers like Whately have appeared to advocate it. Where it originated, I do not know, unless from the frequent comparisons in the Scriptures of death with sleep, which refer solely, I am convinced, to the condition of body, and which are voted down by an overwhelming majority of decided statements relative to the consciousness, happiness, and tangibility of the life into which we immediately pass."

"It is intermediate, in some sense, I suppose."

"It waits between two other conditions, — yes; I think the drift of what we are taught about it leads to that conclusion. I expect to become at once sinless, but to have a broader Christian character many years hence; to be happy at once, but to be happier by and by; to find in myself wonderful new tastes and capacities, which are to be immeasurably ennobled and enlarged after the Resurrection, whatever that may mean."

"What does it mean?"

"I know no more than you, but you shall hear what I think, presently. I was going to say that this seems to be plain enough in the Bible. The angels took Lazarus at once to Abraham. Dives seems to have found no interval between death and consciousness of suffering."

"They always tell you that that is only a parable."

"But it must mean *something*. No story in the Bible has been pulled to pieces and twisted about as that has been. We are in danger of pulling and twisting all sense out of it. Then Judas, having hanged his wretched self, went to his own place. Besides, there was Christ's promise to the thief."

I told her that I had heard Dr. Bland say that we could not place much dependence on that passage, because "Paradise" did not necessarily mean heaven.

"But it meant living, thinking, enjoying; for 'To-day thou shalt *be with me*.' Paul's beautiful perplexed revery, however, would be enough if it stood alone; for he did not know whether he would rather stay in this world, or depart and be with Christ, which is far better. *With Christ*, you see; and His three mysterious days, which typify our intermediate state, were over then, and he had ascended to his Father. Would it be 'far better' either to leave this actual tangible life throbbing with hopes and passions, to leave its busy, Christ-like working, its quiet joys, its very sorrows which are near and human, for a nap of several ages, or even for a vague, lazy, half-alive, disembodied existence?"

"Disembodied? I supposed, of course, that it was disembodied."

"I do not think so. And that brings us to the Resurrection. All the *tendency* of Revelation is to show that an embodied state is superior to a disembodied one. Yet certainly we who love God are promised that death will lead us into a condition which shall have the advantage of this: for the good apostle to die 'was gain.' I don't believe, for instance, that Adam and Eve have been wandering about in a misty condition all these thousands of years. I suspect that we have some sort of body immediately after passing out of this, but that there is to come a mysterious change, equivalent, perhaps, to a re-embodiment, when our capacities for action will be greatly improved, and that in some manner this new form will be connected with this 'garment by the soul laid by.'"

"Deacon Quirk expects to rise in his own entire, original

body, after it has lain in the First Church cemetery a proper number of years, under a black slate headstone, adorned by a willow, and such a 'cherubim' as that poor boy shot, — by the way, if I've laughed at that story once, I have fifty times."

"Perhaps Deacon Quirk would admire a work of art that I found stowed away on the top of your Uncle Calvin's book-cases. It was an old woodcut — nobody knows how old — of an interesting skeleton rising from his grave, and, in a sprightly and modest manner, drawing on his skin, while Gabriel, with apoplectic cheeks, feet uppermost in the air, was blowing a good-sized tin trumpet in his ear!

"No; some of the popular notions of resurrection are simple physiological impossibilities, from causes 'too tedious to specify.' Imagine, for instance, the resurrection of two Hottentots, one of whom has happened to make a dinner of the other some fine day. A little complication there! Or picture the touching scene, when that devoted husband, King Mausolas, whose widow had him burned and ate the ashes, should feel moved to institute a search for his body! It is no wonder that the infidel argument has the best of it, when we attempt to enforce a natural impossibility. It is worth while to remember that Paul expressly stated that we shall *not* rise in our entire earthly bodies. The simile which he used is the seed sown, dying in, and mingling with, the ground. How many of its original particles are found in the full-grown corn?"

"Yet you believe that *something* belonging to this body is preserved for the completion of another?"

"Certainly. I accept God's statement about it, which is as plain as words can make a statement. I do not know, and I do not care to know, how it is to be effected. God will not be at a loss for a way, any more than he is at a loss for a way to make his fields blossom every spring. For aught we know, some invisible compound of an annihilated body may hover, by a divine decree, around the site of death till it is wanted, — sufficient to preserve identity as strictly as a body can ever be said to preserve it; and stranger things have happened. You remember the old Mohammedan belief in the one little bone which is imperishable. Prof. Bush's idea of our triune existence is suggestive, for a notion.[10] He believed, you know, that it takes a material body, a spiritual body, and a soul, to make a man. The spiritual body is enclosed within the material, the soul within the spiritual. Death is simply the slipping off of the outer body, as a husk slips off from its kernel. The deathless frame stands ready then for the soul's untrammelled occupation. But it is a waste of time to speculate over such useless fancies, while so many remain that will vitally affect our happiness."

It is singular; but I never gave a serious thought — and I have done some thinking about other matters — to my heavenly body, till that moment, while I sat listening to her. In fact, till Roy went, the Future was a miserable, mysterious blank, to be drawn on and on in eternal and joyless monotony, and to which, at times, annihilation seemed preferable. I remember, when I was a child, asking father once, if I were so good that I *had* to go to heaven, whether, after a hundred years, God would not let me "die out." More or less of the disposition of that same desperate little sinner I suspect has always clung to me. So I asked Aunt Winifred, in some perplexity, what she supposed our bodies would be like.

"It must be nearly all 'suppose,' " she said, "for we are nowhere definitely told. But this is certain. They will be as real as these."

"But these you can see, you can touch."

"What would be the use of having a body that you can't see and touch? A body is a *body*, not a spirit. Why should you

[10] George Bush (1796–1859), Professor of Hebrew at New York University, was a Presbyterian clergyman who became a Swedenborgian and a spiritualist. The allusion is to Bush's *Anastasis: or, the Doctrine of the Resurrection of the Body, Rationally and Scripturally Considered* (1844).

not, having seen Roy's old smile and heard his own voice, clasp his hand again, and feel his kiss on your happy lips?

"It is really amusing," she continued, "to sum up the notions that good people — excellent people — even thinking people — have of the heavenly body. Vague visions of floating about in the clouds, of balancing — with a white robe on, perhaps — in stiff rows about a throne, like the angels in the old pictures, converging to an apex, or ranged in semi-circles like so many marbles. Murillo has one charming exception. I always take a secret delight in that little cherub of his, kicking the clouds in the right-hand upper corner of the Immaculate Conception; he seems to be having a good time of it, in genuine baby-fashion. The truth is, that the ordinary idea, if sifted accurately, reduces our eternal personality to — *gas*.

"Isaac Taylor holds, that, as far as the abstract idea of spirit is concerned, it may just as reasonably be granite as ether.[11]

"Mrs. Charles says a pretty thing about this.[12] She thinks these 'super-spiritualized angels' very 'unsatisfactory' beings, and that 'the heart returns with loving obstinacy to the young men in long white garments' who sat waiting in the sepulchre.

"Here again I cling to my conjecture about the word 'angel'; for then we should learn emphatically something about our future selves.

" 'As the angels in heaven,' or 'equal unto the angels,' we are told in another place, — that may mean simply what it says. At least, if we are to resemble them in the particular respect of which the words were spoken, — and that one of the most important which could well be selected, — it is not unreasonable to infer that we shall resemble them in others. 'In

---

[11] Isaac Taylor (1787–1865), English author and student of the church fathers. His *Physical Theory of Another Life* (1836) is frequently quoted in *The Gates Ajar*.

[12] Elizabeth Rundle Charles (1828–1896), English writer whose most famous work, *Chronicles of the Schönberg-Cotta Family* (1863) is a fictionalized account of Martin Luther's life and times.

the Resurrection,' by the way, means, in that connection and in many others, simply future state of existence, without any reference to the time at which the great bodily change is to come.

" 'But this is a digression,' as the novelists say. I was going to say, that it bewilders me to conjecture where students of the Bible have discovered the usual foggy nonsense about the corporeity of heaven.

"If there is anything laid down in plain statement, devoid of metaphor or parable, simple and unequivocal, it is the definite contradiction of all that. Paul, in his preface to that sublime apostrophe to death, repeats and reiterates it, lest we should make a mistake in his meaning.

" 'There are celestial *bodies*.' 'It is raised a spiritual *body*.' 'There is a spiritual *body*.' 'It *is* raised in incorruption.' 'It *is* raised in glory.' 'It *is* raised in power.' Moses, too, when he came to the transfigured mount in glory, had as real a *body* as when he went into the lonely mount to die."

"But they will be different from these?"

"The glory of the terrestrial is one, the glory of the celestial another. Take away sin and sickness and misery, and that of itself would make difference enough."

"You do not suppose that we shall look as we look now?"

"I certainly do. At least, I think it more than possible that the 'human form divine,' or something like it, is to be retained. Not only from the fact that risen Elijah bore it; and Moses, who, if he had not passed through his resurrection, does not seem to have looked different from the other, — I have to use those two poor prophets on all occasions, but, as we are told of them neither by parable nor picture, they are important, — and that angels never appeared in any other, but because, in sinless Eden, God chose it for Adam and Eve. What came in unmarred beauty direct from His hand cannot be unworthy of His other Paradise 'beyond the stars.' It would chime in pleasantly, too, with the idea of Redemption, that our very bodies, free from all the distortion of guilt, shall return to something akin to the pure ideal in which He moulded them. Then there is another reason, and stronger."

"What is that?"

"The human form has been borne and dignified forever by Christ. And, further than that, he ascended to His Father in it, and lives there in it as human God to-day."

I had never thought of that, and said so.

"Yes, with the very feet which trod the dusty road to Emmaus; the very wounded hands which Thomas touched, believing; the very lips which ate of the broiled fish and honeycomb; the very voice which murmured 'Mary!' in the garden, and which told her that he ascended unto His Father and her Father, to His God and her God, He 'was parted from them,' and was 'received up into heaven.' His death and resurrection stand forever the great prototype of ours. Otherwise, what is the meaning of such statements as these: 'When He shall appear, we shall be *like Him*'; The first man (Adam) is of the earth; the second man is the Lord. As we have borne the image of the earthy, *we shall also bear the image of the heavenly*'? And what of this, when we are told that our 'vile bodies,' being changed, shall be fashioned *like unto his glorious body*'?"

I asked her if she inferred from that, that we should have just such bodies as the freedom from pain and sin would make of these.

"Flesh and blood cannot inherit the kingdom," she said. "There is no escaping that, even if I had the smallest desire to escape it, which I have not. Whatever is essentially earthly and temporary in the arrangements of this world will be out of place and unnecessary there. Earthly and temporary flesh and blood certainly are."

"Christ said 'A spirit hath not flesh and bones, as ye see me have.'

"A *spirit* hath not; and who ever said that it did? His body had something that appeared like them, certainly. That passage, by the way, has led some ingenious writer on the Chemistry of Heaven to infer that our bodies there will be like these, minus *blood!* I don't propose to spend my time over such investigations. Summing up the meaning of the story of those last days before the Ascension, and granting the shade of mystery which hangs over them, I gather this, — that the spiritual body is real, is tangible, is visible, is human, but that 'we shall be changed.' Some indefinable but thorough change had come over Him. He could withdraw Himself from the recognition of Mary, and from the disciples, whose 'eyes were holden,' as it pleased Him. He came and went through barred and bolted doors. He appeared suddenly in a certain place, without sound of footstep or flutter of garment to announce His approach. He vanished, and was not, like a cloud. New and wonderful powers had been given to Him, of which, probably, His little bewildered group of friends saw but a few illustrations.

"And He was yet *man?*"

"He was Jesus of Nazareth until the sorrowful drama of human life that He had taken upon Himself was thoroughly finished, from manger to sepulchre, and from sepulchre to the right hand of His Father."

"I like to wonder," she said, presently, "what we are going to look like and be like. *Ourselves*, in the first place. 'It is I Myself,' Christ said. Then to be perfectly well, never a sense of pain or weakness, — imagine how much solid comfort, if one had no other, in being forever rid of all the ills that flesh is heir to! Beautiful, too, I suppose we shall be, every one. Have you never had that come over you, with a thrill of compassionate thankfulness, when you have seen a poor girl shrinking, as only girls can shrink, under the life-long affliction of a marred face or form? The loss or presence of beauty is not as slight a deprivation or blessing as the moralists would make it out. Your grandmother, who was the most beautiful woman

I ever saw, the belle of the county all her young days, and the model for artists' fancy sketching even in her old ones, as modest as a violet and as honest as the sunshine, used to have the prettiest little way when we girls were in our teens, and she thought that we must be lectured a bit on youthful vanity, of adding, in her quiet voice, smoothing down her black silk apron as she spoke, 'But still it is a thing to be thankful for, my dear, to have a *comely countenance.*'

"But to return to the track and our future bodies. We shall find them vastly convenient, undoubtedly with powers of which there is no dreaming. Perhaps they will be so one with the soul that to will will be to do, hindrance out of the question. I, for instance, sitting here by you, and thinking that I should like to be in Kansas, would be there. There is an interesting bit of a hint in Daniel about Gabriel, who, 'being caused to fly swiftly, touched him about the time of the evening oblation.' "

"But do you not make a very material kind of heaven out of such suppositions?"

"It depends upon what you mean by 'material.' The term does not, to my thinking, imply degradation, except so far as it is associated with sin. Dr. Chalmers has the right of it, when he talks about *'spiritual materialism.'* He says in his sermon on the New Heavens and Earth, — which, by the way, you should read, and from which I wish a few more of our preachers would learn something, — that we 'forget that on the birth of materialism, when it stood out in the freshness of those glories which the great Architect of Nature had impressed upon it, that then the "morning stars sang together, and all the sons of God shouted for joy." ' I do not believe in a *gross* heaven, but I believe in a *reasonable* one."

4th.

We have been devoting ourselves to feminine vanities all

day out in the orchard. Aunt Winifred has been making her summer bonnet, and I some linen collars. I saw, though she said nothing, that she thought the *crêpe* a little gloomy, and I am going to wear these in the mornings to please her.

She has an accumulation of work on hand, and in the afternoon I offered to tuck a little dress for Faith, — the prettiest pink *barège* affair pale as a blush rose, and about as delicate. Faith, who had been making mud-pies in the swamp, and was spattered with black peat from curls to stockings, looked on approvingly, and wanted it to wear on a flag-root expedition to-morrow. It seemed to do me good to do something for somebody after all this lonely and — I suspect — selfish idleness.

6th.

I read a little of Dr. Chalmers to-day, and went laughing to Aunt Winifred with the first sentence.

"There is a limit to the revelations of the Bible about futurity, and it were a mental or spiritual trespass to go beyond it."

"Ah! but," she said, "look a little farther down."

And I read, "But while we attempt not to be 'wise above that which is written,' we should attempt, and that most studiously, to be wise *up to* that which is written."

8th.

It occurred to me to-day, that it was a noticeable fact, that, among all the visits of angels to this world of which we are told, no one seems to have discovered in any the presence of a dead friend. If redeemed men are subject to the same laws as they, why did such a thing never happen? I asked Aunt Winifred, and she said that the question reminded her of St. Augustine's lonely cry thirty years after the death of Monica: "Ah, the dead do not come back; for, had it been possible, there has not been a night when I should not have seen my mother!" There seemed to be two reasons, she said, why there should be no exceptions to the law of silence imposed between us and those who have left us; one of which was, that we should be overpowered with familiar curiosity about them, which nobody seems to have dared to express in the presence of angels, and the secrets of their life God has decreed that it is unlawful to utter.

"But Lazarus, and Jairus's little daughter, and the dead raised at the Crucifixion, — what of them?" I asked.

"I cannot help conjecturing that they were suffered to forget their glimpse of spiritual life," she said. "Since their resurrection was a miracle, there might be a miracle throughout. At least, their lips must have been sealed, for not a word of their testimony has been saved. When Lazarus dined with Simon, after he had come back to life, — and of that feast we have a minute account in every Gospel, — nobody seems to have asked, or he to have answered, any questions about it.

"The other reason is a sorrowfully sufficient one. It is that *every* lost darling has not gone to heaven. Of all the mercies that our Father has given, this blessed uncertainty, this long unbroken silence, may be the dearest. Bitterly hard for you and me, but what are thousands like you and me weighed against one who stands beside a hopeless grave? Think a minute what mourners there have been, and *whom* they have mourned! Ponder one such solitary instance as that of Vittoria Colonna, wondering, through her widowed years, if she could ever be 'good enough' to join wicked Pescara in another world! This poor earth holds — God only knows how many, God make them very few! — Vittorias. Ah, Mary, what right have *we* to complain?"

9th.

To-night Aunt Winifred had callers, — Mrs. Quirk and (O Homer aristocracy!) the butcher's wife, — and it fell to my lot to put Faith to bed.

The little maiden seriously demurred. Cousin Mary was very good, — O yes, she was good enough, — but her mamma was a great deal gooder; and why could n't little peoples sit up till nine o'clock as well as big peoples, she should like to know! Finally, she came to the gracious conclusion that perhaps I'd *do*, made me carry her all the way up stairs, and dropped, like a little lump of lead, half asleep on my shoulder, before two buttons were unfastened.

Feeling under some sort of theological obligation to hear her say her prayers, I pulled her curls a little till she awoke, and went through with "Now I lay me down to sleep, I pway ve Lord," triumphantly. I supposed that was the end, but it seems that she has been also taught the Lord's Prayer, which she gave me promptly to understand.

"O, see here! That is n't all. I can say Our Father, and you've got to help me a lot!"

This very soon became a self-evident proposition; but by our united efforts we managed, after tribulations manifold, to arrive successfully at "For ever'n' ever'n' ever'n' *A*-men."

"Dear me," she said, jumping up with a yawn. "I think that's a *dreadful long-tailed prayer*, — don't you, Cousin Mary?"

"Now I must kiss mamma good night," she announced, when she was tucked up at last.

"But mamma kissed you good night before you came up."

"O, so she did. Yes, I 'member. Well, it's papa I've got to kiss. I knew there was somebody."

I looked at her in perplexity.

"Why, there!" she said, "in the upper drawer, — my pretty little papa in a purple frame. Don't you know?"

I went to the bureau-drawer, and found in a case of velvet a small ivory painting of her father. This I brought, wondering, and the child took it reverently and kissed the pictured lips.

"Faith," I said, as I laid it softly back, "do you always do this?"

"Do what? Kiss papa good night? O yes, I've done that ever since I was a little girl, you know. I guess I've always kissed him pretty much. When I'm a naughty girl he feels *real* sorry. He's gone to heaven. I like him. O yes, and then, when I'm through kissing, mamma kisses him too."

X

June 11.

I was in her room this afternoon while she was dressing. I like to watch her brush her beautiful gray hair; it quite alters her face to have it down; it seems to shrine her in like a cloud, and the outlines of her cheeks round out, and she grows young.

"I used to be proud of my hair when I was a girl," she said with a slight blush, as she saw me looking at her; "it was all I had to be vain of, and I made the most of it. Ah well! I was dark-haired three years ago.

"O you regular old woman!" she added, smiling at herself in the mirror, as she twisted the silver coils flashing through her fingers. "Well, when I am in heaven, I shall have my pretty brown hair again."

It seemed odd enough to hear that; then the next minute it did not seem odd at all, but the most natural thing in the world.

June 14.

She said nothing to me about the anniversary and, though it has been in my thoughts all the time, I said nothing to her. I thought that she would shut herself up for the day, and was rather surprised that she was about as usual busily at work, chatting with me, and playing with Faith. Just after tea, she went away alone for a time, and came back a little quiet, but that was all. I was for some reason impressed with the feeling that she kept the day in memory, not so much as the day of her mourning as of his release.

Longing to do something for her, yet not knowing what to do, I went into the garden while she was away, and, finding some carnations, that shone like stars in the dying light, I gathered them all, and took them to her room, and, filling my tiny porphyry vase, left them on the bracket, under the photograph of Uncle Forceythe that hangs by the window.

When she found them, she called me, and kissed me. "Thank you, dear," she said, "and thank God too, Mary, for me. That he should have been happy, — happy and out of pain, for three long beautiful years! O, think of that!"

When I was in her room with the flowers, I passed the table on which her little Bible lay open. A mark of rich ribbon — a black ribbon — fell across the pages; it bore in silver text these words: —

"Thou shalt have no other gods before me."

20th.

"I thank thee, my God, the river of Lethe may indeed flow through the Elysian Fields, — it does not water the Christian's Paradise."

Aunt Winifred was saying that over to herself in a dreamy undertone this morning, and I happened to hear her.

"Just a quotation, dear," she said, smiling, in answer to my look of inquiry, "I could n't originate so pretty a thing. *Is n't it pretty?*"

"Very; but I am not sure that I understand it."

"You thought that forgetfulness would be necessary to happiness?"

"Why, — yes; as far as I had ever thought about it; that is, after our last ties with this world are broken. It does not seem

to me that I could be happy to remember all that I have suffered and all that I have sinned here."

"But the last of all the sins will be as if it had never been.
Christ takes care of that. No shadow of a sense of guilt can
dog you, or affect your relations to Him or your other friends.
The last pain borne, the last tear, the last sigh, the last lonely
hour, the last unsatisfied dream, forever gone by; why should
not the dead past bury its dead?"

"Then why remember it?"

" 'Save but to swell the sense of being blest.' Besides, forgetfulness of the disagreeable things of this life implies forgetfulness of the pleasant ones. They are all tangled together."

"To be sure. I don't know that I should like that."

"Of course you would n't. Imagine yourself in a state of being where you and Roy had lost your past; all that you had
borne and enjoyed, and hoped and feared, together; the pretty
little memories of your babyhood, and first 'half-days' at
school, when he used to trudge along beside you, — little fellow! how many times I have watched him! — holding you
tight by the apron-sleeve or hat-string, or bits of fat fingers,
lest you should run away or fall. Then the old Academy
pranks, out of which you used to help each other; his little
chivalry and elder-brotherly advice; the mischief in his eyes;
some of the 'Sunday-night talks'; the first novel that you read
and dreamed over together; the college stories; the chats over
the corn-popper by firelight; the earliest, earnest looking-on
into life together, its temptations conquered, its lessons
learned, its disappointments faced together, — always you
two, — would you like to, are you *likely* to, forget all this?

"Roy might as well be not Roy, but a strange angel, if you
should. Heaven will be not less heaven, but more, for this
pleasant remembering. So many other and greater and happier
memories will fill up the time then, that after years these things
may — probably will — seem smaller than it seems to us now

they can ever be; but they will, I think, be always dear; just as we look back to our baby-selves with a pitying sort of fondness, and, though the little creatures are of small enough use to us now, yet we like to keep good friends with them for old times' sake.

"I have no doubt that you and I shall sit down some summer afternoon in heaven and talk over what we have been saying to-day, and laugh perhaps at all the poor little dreams we have been dreaming of what has not entered into the heart of man. You see it is certain to be so much *better* than anything that I can think of; which is the comfort of it. And Roy —"

"Yes, some more about Roy, please."

"Supposing he were to come right into the room now, — and I slipped out, — and you had him all to yourself again — Now, dear, don't cry, but wait a minute!" Her caressing hand fell on my hair. "I did not mean to hurt you, but to say that your first talk with him, after you stand face to face, may be like that.

"Remembering this life is going to help us amazingly, I fancy, to appreciate the next," she added, by way of period. "Christ seems to have thought so, when he called to the minds of those happy people what, in that unconscious ministering of lowly faith which may never reap its sheaf in the field where the seed was sown, they had not had the comfort of finding out before, — 'I was sick and in prison, and ye visited me.' And to come again to Abraham in the parable, did he not say, 'Son, *remember* that thou in thy lifetime hadst good things and Lazarus evil'?"

"I wonder what it is going to look like," I said, as soon as I could put poor Dives out of my mind.

"Heaven? Eye hath not seen, but I have my fancies. I think I want some mountains, and very many trees."

"Mountains and trees!"

"Yes; mountains as we see them at sunset and sunrise, or

when the maples are on fire and there are clouds enough to
make great purple shadows chase each other into lakes of light,
over the tops and down the sides, — the *ideal* of mountains
which we catch in rare glimpses, as we catch the ideal of
everything. Trees as they look when the wind cooes through
them on a June afternoon; elms or lindens or pines as cool as
frost, and yellow sunshine trickling through on moss. Trees
in a forest so thick that it shuts out the world, and you walk
like one in a sanctuary. Trees pierced by stars, and trees in a
bath of summer moons to which the thrill of 'Love's young
dream' shall cling forever — But there is no end to one's fancies. Some water, too, I would like."

"There shall be no more sea."

"Perhaps not; though, as the sea is the great type of separation and of destruction, that may be only figurative. But I'm
not particular about the sea, if I can have rivers and little
brooks, and fountains of just the right sort; the fountains of
this world don't please me generally. I want a little brook to
sit and sing to Faith by. O, I forgot! she will be a large girl
probably, won't she?"

"Never too large to like to hear your mother sing, will you,
Faith?"

"O no," said Faith, who bobbed in and out again like a
canary just then, — "not unless I'm *dreadful* big, with long
dresses and a waterfall, you know. I s'pose, maybe, I'd have to
have little girls myself to sing to, then. I hope they'll behave
better'n Mary Ann does. She's lost her other arm, and all her
sawdust is just running out. Besides, Kitty thought she was
a mouse, and ran down cellar with her, and she's all shooken
up, somehow. She don't look very pretty."

"Flowers too," her mother went on, after the interruption.
"*Not* all amaranth and asphodel, but of variety and color and
beauty unimagined; glorified lilies of the valley, heavenly tea-
rose buds, and spiritual harebells among them. O, how your

poor mother used to say, — you know flowers were her poetry, — coming in weak and worn from her garden in the early part of her sickness, hands and lap and basket full: 'Winifred, if I only supposed I *could* have some flowers in heaven I should n't be half so afraid to go!' I had not thought as much about these things then as I have now, or I should have known better how to answer her. I should like, if I had my choice, to have day-lilies and carnations fresh under my windows all the time."

"Under your windows?"

"Yes. I hope to have a home of my own."

"Not a house?"

"Something not unlike it. In the Father's house are many mansions. Sometimes I fancy that those words have a literal meaning which the simple men who heard them may have understood better than we, and that Christ is truly 'preparing' my home for me. He must be there, too, you see, — I mean John."

I believe that gave me some thoughts that I ought not to have, and so I made no reply.

"If we have trees and mountains and flowers and books," she went on, smiling, "I don't see why not have houses as well. Indeed, they seem to me as supposable as anything can be which is guess-work at the best; for what a homeless, desolate sort of sensation it gives one to think of people wandering over the 'sweet fields beyond the flood' without a local habitation and a name. What could be done with the millions who, from the time of Adam, have been gathering there, unless they lived under the conditions of organized society? Organized society involves homes, not unlike the homes of this world.

"What other arrangement could be as pleasant, or could be pleasant at all? Robertson's definition of a church exactly fits. 'More united in each other, because more united in

God.' [13] A happy home is the happiest thing in the world. I do not see why it should not be in any world. I do not believe that all the little tendernesses of family ties are thrown by and lost with this life. In fact, Mary, I cannot think that anything which has in it the elements of permanency is to be lost, but sin. Eternity cannot be — it cannot be the great blank ocean which most of us have somehow or other been brought up to feel that it is, which shall swallow up, in a pitiless, glorified way, all the little brooks of our delight. So I expect to have my beautiful home, and my husband, and Faith, as I had them here; with many differences and great ones, but *mine* just the same. Unless Faith goes into a home of her own, — the little creature! I suppose she can't always be a baby.

"Do you remember what a pretty little wistful way Charles Lamb has of wondering about all this?

" 'Shall I enjoy friendships there, wanting the smiling indications which point me to them here, — "the sweet assurance of a look"? Sun, and sky, and breeze, and solitary walks, and summer holidays, and the greenness of fields, and the delicious juices of meats and fish, and society, ... and candle-light and fireside conversations, and innocent vanities, and jests, and *irony itself*, — do these things go out with life?' "

"Now, Aunt Winifred!" I said, sitting up straight, "what am I to do with these beautiful heresies? If Deacon Quirk *should* hear!"

"I do not see where the heresy lies. As I hold fast by the Bible, I cannot be in much danger."

"But you don't glean your conjectures from the Bible."

"I conjecture nothing that the Bible contradicts. I do not believe as truth indisputable anything that the Bible does not

[13] Frederick William Robertson (1816–1853), an eloquent preacher, drew many Oxford undergraduates to his parish in the poorest part of town. The sermons he preached to the laboring classes in Trinity Chapel, Brighton, emphasize the humanity of Christ. Stopford Brooke published Robertson's *Life and Letters* (1865).

give me. But I reason from analogy about this, as we all do about other matters. Why should we not have pretty things in heaven? If this 'bright and beautiful economy' of skies and rivers, of grass and sunshine, of hills and valleys, is not too good for such a place as this world, will there be any less variety of the bright and beautiful in the next? There is no reason for supposing that the voice of God will speak to us in thunder-claps, or that it will not take to itself the thousand gentle, suggestive tongues of a nature built on the ruins of this, an unmarred system of beneficence.

"There is a pretty argument in the fact that just such sunrises, such opening of buds, such fragrant dropping of fruit, such bells in the brooks, such dreams at twilight, and such hush of stars, were fit for Adam and Eve, made holy man and woman. How do we know that the abstract idea of a heaven needs imply anything very much unlike Eden? There is some reason as well as poetry in the conception of a 'Paradise Regained.' A 'new earth wherein dwelleth righteousness.'"

"But how far is it safe to trust to this kind of argument?"

"Bishop Butler will answer you better than I. Let me see, — Isaac Taylor says something about that."

She went to the bookcase for his "Physical Theory of Another Life," and, finding her place, showed me this passage: —

"If this often repeated argument from analogy is to be termed, as to the conclusions it involves, a conjecture merely, we ought then to abandon altogether every kind of abstract reasoning; nor will it be easy afterwards to make good any principle of natural theology. In truth, the very basis of reasoning is shaken by a scepticism so sweeping as this."

And in another place: —

"None need fear the consequences of such endeavors who have well learned the prime principle of sound philosophy, namely, not to allow the most plausible and pleasing conjectures to unsettle our convictions of truth . . . . resting upon positive evidence. If there be any who frown upon all such

attempts, ... they would do well to consider, that although individually, and from the constitution of their minds,
they may find it very easy to abstain from every path of ex-
cursive meditation, it is not so with others who almost irre-
sistibly are borne forward to the vast field of universal con-
templation, — a field from which the human mind is not to
be barred, and which is better taken possession of by those
who reverently bow to the authority of Christianity, than left
open to impiety."

"Very good," I said, laying down the book. "But about
those trees and houses, and the rest of your 'pretty things'?
Are they to be like these?"

"I don't suppose that the houses will be made of oak and
pine and nailed together, for instance. But I hope for heavenly
types of nature and of art. *Something that will be to us then
what these are now.* That is the amount of it. They may be
as 'spiritual' as you please; they will answer all the purpose
to us. As we are not spiritual beings yet, however, I am under
the necessity of calling them by their earthly names. You remember Plato's old theory, that the ideal of everything exists
eternally in the mind of God. If that is so, — and I do not see
how it can be otherwise, — then whatever of God is expressed
to us in this world by flower, or blade of grass, or human
face, why should not that be expressed forever in heaven by
something corresponding to flower, or grass, or human face?
I do not mean that the heavenly creation will be less real than
these, but more so. Their 'spirituality' is of such a sort that
our gardens and forests and homes are but shadows of them.

"You don't know how I amuse myself at night thinking
this all over before I go to sleep; wondering what one thing
will be like, and another thing; planning what I should like;
thinking that John has seen it all, and wondering if he is
laughing at me because I know so little about it. I tell you,
Mary, there's a 'deal o' comfort in 't,' as Phoebe says about
her cup of tea."

July 5.

Aunt Winifred has been hunting up a Sunday-school class for herself and one for me; which is a venture that I never was persuaded into undertaking before. She herself is fast becoming acquainted with the poorer people of the town.

I find that she is a thoroughly busy Christian, with a certain "week-day holiness" that is strong and refreshing, like a west wind. Church-going, and conversations on heaven, by no means exhaust her vitality.

She told me a pretty thing about her class; it happened the first Sabbath that she took it. Her scholars are young girls of from fourteen to eighteen years of age, children of church-members, most of them. She seemed to have taken their hearts by storm. *She* says, "They treated me very prettily, and made me love them at once."

Clo Bentley is in the class; Clo is a pretty, soft-eyed little creature, with a shrinking mouth, and an absorbing passion for music, which she has always been too poor to gratify. I suspect that her teacher will make a pet of her. She says that in the course of her lesson, or, in her words, —

"While we were all talking together, somebody pulled my sleeve, and there was Clo in the corner, with her great brown eyes fixed on me. 'See here!' she said in a whisper, 'I can't be good! I would be good if I could *only* just have a piano!'

" 'Well, Clo,' I said, 'if you will be a good girl, and go to heaven, I think you will have a piano there, and play just as much as you care to.'

"You ought to have seen the look the child gave me! Delight and fear and incredulous bewilderment tumbled over each other, as if I had proposed taking her into a forbidden fairy-land.

" 'Why, Mrs. Forceythe! Why, they won't let anybody have a piano up there! not in *heaven?*'

"I laid down the question-book, and asked what kind of place she supposed that heaven was going to be.

" 'O,' she said, with a dreary sigh, 'I never think about it when I can help it. I suppose we *shall all just stand there!*'

"And you?" I asked of the next, a bright girl with snapping eyes.

" 'Do you want me to talk good, or tell the truth?' she answered me. Having been given to understand that she was not expected to 'talk good' in my class, she said, with an approving, decided nod: 'Well, then! I don't think it's going to be *anything nice* anyway. No, I don't! I told my last teacher so, and she looked just as shocked, and said I never should go there as long as I felt so. That made me mad, and I told her I did n't see but I should be as well off in one place as another, except for the fire.'

"A silent girl in the corner began at this point to look interested. 'I always supposed,' said she, 'that you just floated round in heaven — you know — all together — something like jujube paste!'

"Whereupon I shut the question-book entirely, and took the talking to myself for a while.

" 'But I *never* thought it was anything like that,' interrupted little Clo, presently, her cheeks flushed with excitement. 'Why, I should like to go, if it is like that! I never supposed people talked, unless it was about converting people, and saying your prayers, and all that.'

"Now, were n't those ideas * alluring and comforting for young girls in the blossom of warm human life? They were trying with all their little hearts to 'be good,' too, some of them, and had all of them been to church and Sunday school all their lives. Never, never, if Jesus Christ had been Teacher and Preacher to them, would He have pictured their blessed endless years with Him in such bleak colors. They are not the hues of his Bible."

* Facts.

❧ XI ❧

July 16.

W E TOOK a trip to-day to East Homer for butter. Neither angels nor principalities could convince Phoebe that any butter but "Stephen David's" might, could, would, or should be used in this family. So to Mr. Stephen David's, a journey of four miles, I meekly betake myself at stated periods in the domestic year, burdened with directions about firkins and half-firkins, pounds and half-pounds, salt and no salt, churning and "working over"; some of which I remember and some of which I forget, and to all of which Phoebe considers me sublimely incapable of attending.

The afternoon was perfect, and we took things leisurely, letting the reins swing from the hook, — an arrangement to which Mr. Tripp's old gray was entirely agreeable, — and, leaning back against the buggy-cushions, wound along among the strong, sweet pine-smells, lazily talking, or lazily silent, as the spirit moved, and as only two people who thoroughly understand and like each other can talk or be silent.

We rode home by Deacon Quirk's, and, as we jogged by, there broke upon our view a blooming vision of the Deacon himself, at work in his potato-field with his son and heir, who, by the way, has the reputation of being the most awkward fellow in the township.

The amiable church-officer, having caught sight of us, left

his work, and coming up to the fence "in rustic modesty un-
scared," guiltless of coat or vest, his calico shirt-sleeves rolled
up to his huge brown elbows, and his dusty straw hat flapping
in the wind, rapped on the rails with his hoe-handle as a sign
for us to stop.

"Are we in a hurry?" I asked, under my breath.

"O no," said Aunt Winifred. "He has somewhat to say
unto me, I see by his eyes. I have been expecting it. Let us
hear him out. Good afternoon, Deacon Quirk."

"Good afternoon, ma'am. Pleasant day?"

She assented to the statement, novel as it was.

"A very pleasant day," repeated the Deacon, looking for
the first time in his life, to my knowledge, a little undecided
as to what he should say next. "Remarkable fine day for riding.
In a hurry?"

"Well, not especially. Did you want anything of me?"

"You're a church-member, are n't you, ma'am?" asked
the Deacon, abruptly.

"I am."

"Orthodox?"

"O yes," with a smile. "You had a reason for asking?"

"Yes, ma'am; I had, as you might say, a reason for asking."

The Deacon laid his hoe on the top of the fence, and his
arms across it, and pushed his hat on the back of his head in
a becoming and argumentative manner.

"I hope you don't consider that I'm taking liberties if I
have a little religious conversation with you, Mrs. Forceythe."

"It is no offence to me if you are," replied Mrs. Forceythe,
with a twinkle in her eye; but both twinkle and words glanced
off from the Deacon.

"My wife was telling me last night," he began, with an omi-
nous cough, "that her niece, Clotildy Bentley, — Moses Bentley's daughter, you know, and one of your sentimental girls
that reads poetry, and is easy enough led away by vain delu-

sions and false doctrine, — was under your charge at Sunday school. Now Clotildy is intimate with my wife, — who is her aunt on her mother's side, and always tries to do her duty by her, — and she told Mrs. Quirk what you'd been a saying to those young minds on the Sabbath."

He stopped, and observed her impressively, as if he expected to see the guilty blushes of arraigned heresy covering her amused, attentive face.

"I hope you will pardon me, ma'am, for repeating it, but Clotildy said that you told her she should have a pianna in heaven. A *pianna*, ma'am!"

"I certainly did," she said, quietly.

"You did? Well, now, I did n't believe it, nor I would n't believe it, till I'd asked you! I thought it warn't more than fair that I should ask you, before repeating it, you know. It's none of my business, Mrs. Forceythe, any more than that I take a general interest in the spiritooal welfare of the youth of our Sabbath school; but I am very much surprised! I am *very* much surprised!"

"I am surprised that you should be, Deacon Quirk. Do you believe that God would take a poor little disappointed girl like Clo, who has been all her life here forbidden the enjoyment of a perfectly innocent taste, and keep her in His happy heaven eternal years, without finding means to gratify it? I don't."

"I tell Clotildy I don't see what she wants of a pianna-forte," observed "Clotildy's" uncle, sententiously. "She can go to singin' school, and she's been in the choir ever since I have, which is six years come Christmas. Besides, I don't think it's our place to speckylate on the mysteries of the heavenly spere. My wife told her that she must n't believe any such things as that, which were very irreverent, and contrary to the Scriptures, and Clo went home crying. She said, 'It was so pretty to think about.' It is very easy to impress these delusions of fancy on the young."

"Pray, Deacon Quirk," said Aunt Winifred, leaning earnestly forward in the carriage, "will you tell me what there is 'irreverent' or 'unscriptural' in the idea that there will be instrumental music in heaven?"

"Well," replied the Deacon, after some consideration, "come to think of it, there will be harps, I suppose. Harpers harping with their harps on the sea of glass. But I don't believe there will be any piannas. It's a dreadfully material way to talk about that glorious world, to my thinking."

"If you could show me wherein a harp is less 'material' than a piano, perhaps I should agree with you."

Deacon Quirk looked rather nonplussed for a minute.

"What *do* you suppose people will do in heaven?" she asked again.

"Glorify God," said the Deacon, promptly recovering himself, — "glorify God, and sing Worthy the Lamb! We shall be clothed in white robes with palms in our hands, and bow before the Great White Throne. We shall be engaged in such employments as befit sinless creatures in a spiritooal state of existence."

"Now, Deacon Quirk," replied Aunt Winifred, looking him over from head to foot, — old straw hat, calico shirt, blue overalls, and cowhide boots, coarse, work-worn hands, and "narrow forehead braided tight," — "just imagine yourself, will you? taken out of this life this minute, as you stand here in your potato-field (the Deacon changed his position with evident uneasiness), and put into another life, — not anybody else, but yourself, just as you left this spot, — and do you honestly think that you should be happy to go and put on a white dress and stand still in a choir with a green branch in one hand and a singing-book in the other, and sing and pray and never do anything but sing and pray, this year, next year, and every year forever?"

"We-ell," he replied, surprised into a momentary flash of carnal candor, "I can't say that I should n't wonder for a minute, maybe, *how Abinadab would ever get those potatoes hoed without me.* — Abinadab! go back to your work!"

The graceful Abinadab had sauntered up during the conversation, and was listening, hoe in hand and mouth open. He slunk away when his father spoke, but came up again presently on tiptoe when Aunt Winifred was talking. There was an interested, intelligent look about his square and pitifully embarrassed face, which attracted my notice.

"But then," proceeded the Deacon, re-enforced by the sudden recollection of his duties as a father and a church-member, "that could n't be a permanent state of feeling, you know. I expect to be transformed by the renewing of my mind to appreciate the glories of the New Jerusalem, descending out of heaven from God. That's what I expect, marm. Now I heerd that you told Mrs. Bland, or that Mary told her, or that she heerd it someway, that you said you supposed there were trees and flowers and houses and such in heaven. I told my wife I thought your deceased husband was a Congregational minister, and I did n't believe you ever said it; but that's the rumor."

Without deeming it necessary to refer to her "deceased husband," Aunt Winifred replied that "rumor" was quite right.

"Well!" said the Deacon, with severe significance, "*I* believe in a spiritooal heaven."

I looked him over again, — hat, hoe, shirt, and all; scanned his obstinate old face with its stupid, good eyes and animal mouth. Then I glanced at Aunt Winifred as she leaned forward in the afternoon light; the white, finely cut woman, with her serene smile and rapt, saintly eyes, — every inch of her, body and soul, refined not only by birth and training, but by the long nearness of her heart to Christ.

"Of the earth, earthy. Of the heavens, heavenly." The two faces sharpened themselves into two types. Which, indeed, was the better able to comprehend a "spiritooal heaven"?

"It is distinctly stated in the Bible, by which I suppose we shall both agree," said Aunt Winifred, gently, "that there shall be a *new earth*, as well as new heavens. It is noticeable, also, that the descriptions of heaven, although a series of metaphors, are yet singularly earthlike and tangible ones. Are flowers and skies and trees less 'spiritual' than white dresses and little palm-branches? In fact, where are you going to get your little branches without trees? What could well be more suggestive of material modes of living, and material industry, than a city marked into streets and alleys, paved solidly with gold, walled in and barred with gates whose jewels are named and counted, and whose very length and breadth are measured with a celestial surveyor's chain?"

"But I think we'd ought to stick to what the Bible says," answered the Deacon, stolidly. "If it says golden cities and does n't say flowers, it means cities and does n't mean flowers. I dare say you 're a good woman, Mrs. Forceythe, if you do hold such oncommon doctrine, and I don't doubt you mean well enough, but I don't think that we ought to trouble ourselves about these mysteries of a future state. *I'm* willing to trust them to God!"

The evasion of a fair argument by this self-sufficient spasm of piety was more than I could calmly stand, and I indulged in a subdued explosion, — Auntie says it sounded like Fourth of July crackers touched off under a wet barrel.

"Deacon Quirk! do you mean to imply that Mrs. Forceythe does not trust it to God? The truth is, that the existence of such a world as heaven is a fact from which you shrink. You know you do! She has twenty thoughts about it where you have one; yet you set up a claim to superior spirituality!"

"Mary, Mary, you are a little excited, I fear. God is a spirit, and they that worship him must worship him in spirit and in truth!"

The relevancy of this last, I confess myself incapable of perceiving, but the good man seemed to be convinced that he had made a point, and we rode off leaving him under that blissful delusion.

"If he *were n't* a good man!" I sighed. "But he is, and I must respect him for it."

"Of course you must; nor is he to blame that he is narrow and rough. I should scarcely have argued as seriously as I did with him, but that, as I fancy him to be a representative of a class, I want to try an experiment. Is n't he amusing, though? He is precisely one of Mr. Stopford Brooke's men 'who can understand nothing which is original.'"

"Are there, or are there not, more of such men in our church than in others?"

"Not more proportionately to numbers. But I would not have them thinned out. The better we do Christ's work, the more of uneducated, neglected, or debased mind will be drawn to try and serve Him with us. He sought out the lame, the halt, the blind, the stupid, the crotchety, the rough, as well as the equable, the intelligent, the refined. Untrained Christians in any sect will always have their eccentricities and their littlenesses, at which the silken judgment of high places, where the Carpenter's Son would be a strange guest, will sneer. That never troubles me. It only raises the question in my mind whether cultivated Christians generally are sufficiently *cultivators*, scattering their golden gifts on wayside ground."

"Now take Deacon Quirk," I suggested, when we had ridden along a little way under the low, green arches of the elms, "and put him into heaven as you proposed, just as he is, and what *is* he going to do with himself? He can dig potatoes and sell them without cheating, and give generously of their proceeds to foreign missions; but take away his potatoes, and what would become of him? I don't know a human being more incapacitated to live in such a heaven as he believes in."

"Very true, and a good, common-sense argument against such a heaven. I don't profess to surmise what will be found for him to do, beyond this, — that it will be some very palpable work that he can understand. How do we know that he would not be appointed guardian of his poor son here, to whom I suspect he has not been all that father might be in this life, and that he would not have his body as well as his soul to look after, his farm as well as his prayers? to him might be committed the charge of the dews and the rains and the hundred unseen influences that are at work on this very potato-field."

"But when his son has gone in his turn, and we have all gone, and there are no more potato-fields? An Eternity remains."

"You don't know that there would n't be any potato-fields; there may be some kind of agricultural employments even then. To whomsoever a talent is given, it will be given him wherewith to use it. Besides, by that time the good Deacon will be immensely changed. I suppose that the simple transition of death, which rids him of sin and of grossness, will not only wonderfully refine him, but will have its effect upon his intellect."

"If a talent is given, use will be found for it? Tell me some more about that."

"I fancy many things about it; but of course can feel sure of only the foundation principle. This life is a great school-house. The wise Teacher trains in us such gifts as, if we graduate honorably, will be of most service in the perfect manhood and womanhood that come after. He sees, as we do not, that a power is sometimes best trained by repression. 'We do not always lose an advantage when we dispense with it,' Goethe says. But the suffocated lives, like little Clo's there, make my heart ache sometimes. I take comfort in thinking how they will bud and blossom up in the air, by and by. There are a great many of them. We tread them underfoot in our

careless stepping now and then, and do not see that they have
not the elasticity to rise from our touch. 'Heaven may be a
place for those who failed on earth,' the Country Parson
says." [14]

"Then there will be air enough for all?"

"For all; for those who have had a little bloom in this world,
as well. I suppose the artist will paint his pictures, the poet sing
his happy songs; the orator and author will not find their
talents hidden in the eternal darkness of a grave; the sculptor
will use his beautiful gift in the moulding of some heavenly
Carrara; 'as well the singer as the player on instruments shall
be there.' Christ said a thing that has grown on me with new
meanings lately, — 'He that *loseth his life for my sake shall
find it.' It*, you see, — not another man's life, not a strange
compound of powers and pleasures, but his own familiar
aspirations. So we shall best 'glorify God,' not less there than
here, by doing it in the peculiar way that He himself marked
out for us. But — ah, Mary, you see it is only the life 'lost'
for His sake that shall be so beautifully found. A great man
never goes to heaven because he is great. He must go, as the
meanest of his fellow-sinners go, with face towards Calvary,
and every golden treasure used for love of Him who showed
him how."

"What would the old Pagans — and modern ones, too, for
that matter — say to that? Was n't it Tacitus who announced
it as his belief, that immortality was granted as a special gift
to a few superior minds? For the people who persisted in making up the rest of the world, poor things! as it could be of little
consequence what became of them, they might die as the brute
dieth."

"It seems an unbearable thing to me sometimes," she went

[14] "The Country Parson" was the pen name of the Scottish divine, Andrew Kennedy Hutchinson Boyd, whose *Autumn Holidays of a Country
Parson* (1865), and *Recreations of a Country Parson* (1859, 1861, 1878)
were widely read in America.

on, "the wreck of a gifted soul. A man who can be, if he chooses, as much better and happier than the rest of us as the ocean reflects more sky than a mill-pond, must also be, if he chooses, more wicked and more miserable. It takes longer to reach sea-shells than river-pebbles. I am compelled to think, also, that intellectual rank must in heaven bear some proportion to goodness. There are last and there are first that shall have changed places. As the tree falleth, there shall it lie, and with that amount of holiness of which a man leaves this life the possessor, he must start in another. I have seen great thinkers, 'foremost men' in science, in theology, in the arts, who, I solemnly believe, will turn aside in heaven, — and will turn humbly and heartily, — to let certain day-laborers and paupers whom I have known go up before them as kings and priests unto God."

"I believe that. But I was going to ask, — for poor creatures like your respected niece, who has n't a talent, nor even a single absorbing taste, for one thing above another thing, — what shall she do?"

"Whatever she liketh best; something very useful, my dear, don't be afraid, and very pleasant. Something, too, for which this life has fitted you; though you may not understand how that can be, better than did poor Heine on his 'matrazzen-gruft,' reading all the books that treated of his disease. 'But what good this reading is to do me I don't know,' he said, 'except that it will qualify me to give lectures in heaven on the ignorance of doctors on earth about diseases of the spinal marrow.'"

"I don't know how many times I have thought of — I believe it was the poet Gray, who said that his idea of heaven was to lie on the sofa and read novels. That touches the lazy part of us, though."

"Yes, they will be the active, outgoing, generous elements of our nature that will be brought into use then, rather than the self-centred and dreamy ones. Though I suppose that we shall read in heaven, — being influenced to be better and nobler by good and noble teachers of the pen, not less there than here."

"O think of it? To have books, and music, — and pictures?"

"All that Art, 'the handmaid of the Lord,' can do for us, I have no doubt will be done. Eternity will never become monotonous. Variety without end, charms unnumbered within charms, will be devised by Infinite ingenuity to minister to our delight. Perhaps, — this is just my fancying, — perhaps there will be whole planets turned into galleries of art, over which we may wander at will; or into orchestral halls where the highest possibilities of music will be realized to singer and to hearer. Do you know, I have sometimes had a flitting notion that music would be the language of heaven? It certainly differs in some indescribable manner from the other arts. We have most of us felt it in our different ways. It always seems to me like the cry of a great, sad life dragged to use in this world against its will. Pictures and statues and poems fit themselves to their work more contentedly. Symphony and song struggle in fetters. That sense of conflict is not good for me. It is quite as likely to harm as to help. Then perhaps the mysteries of sidereal systems will be spread out like a child's map before us. Perhaps we shall take journeys to Jupiter and to Saturn and to the glittering haze of nebulæ, and to the site of ruined worlds whose 'extinct light is yet travelling through space.' Occupation for explorers there, you see!"

"You make me say with little Clo, 'O, why, I want to go!' every time I hear you talk. But there is one thing, — you spoke of families living together."

"Yes."

"And you spoke of — your husband. But the Bible — "

"Says there shall be no marrying nor giving in marriage. I know that. Nor will there be such marrying or giving in marriage as there is in a world like this. Christ expressly goes on to state, that we shall be *as* the angels in heaven. How do we know what heavenly unions of heart with heart exist among the angels? It leaves me margin enough to live and be happy with John forever, and it holds many possibilities for the settlement of all perplexing questions brought about by the relations of this world. It is of no use to talk much about them. But it is on that very verse that I found my unshaken belief that they will be smoothed out in some natural and happy way, with which each one shall be content."

"But O, there is a great gulf fixed; and on one side one, and on the other another, and they loved each other."

Her face paled, — it always pales, I notice, at the mention of this mystery, — but her eyes never lost by a shade their steadfast trust.

"Mary, don't question me about *that*. That belongs to the unutterable things. God will take care of it. I *think* I could leave it to Him even if he brought it for me myself to face. I feel sure that He will make it all come out right. Perhaps He will be so dear to us, that we could not love any one who hated Him. In some way the void *must* be filled, for He shall wipe away tears. But it seems to me that the only thought in which there can be any *rest*, and in that there *can*, is this: that Christ, who loves us even as His Father loves Him, can be happy in spite of the existence of a hell. If it is possible to Him, surely He can make it possible to us."

"Two things that He has taught us," she said after a silence, "give me beautiful assurance that none of these dreams with which I help myself can be beyond His intention to fulfil. One is, that eye hath not seen it, nor ear heard it, nor the heart conceived it, — this lavishness of reward which He is keeping for us. Another is, that 'I shall be *satisfied* when I awake.'"

"With his likeness."

"With his likeness. And about that I have other things to say."

But Old Gray stopped at the gate and Phoebe was watching for her butter, and it was no time to say them then.

◆ XII ◆

Aunt Winifred has connected herself with our church. I think it was rather hard for her, breaking the last tie that bound her to her husband's people; but she had a feeling, that, if her work is to be done and her days ended here, she had better take up all such little threads of influence to make herself one with us.

To-day what should Deacon Quirk do but make a solemn call on Mrs. Forceythe, for the purpose of asking — and this with a hint that he wished he had asked before she became a member of the Homer First Congregational Church — whether there were truth in the rumors, now rife about town, that she was a Swedenborgian!

Aunt Winifred broke out laughing, and laughed merrily. The Deacon frowned.

"I used to fancy that I believed in Swedenborg," she said, as soon as she could sober down a little.

The Deacon pricked up his ears, with visions of excommunications and councils reflected on every feature.

"Until I read his books," she finished.

"Oh!" said the Deacon. He waited for more, but she seemed to consider the conversation at an end.

"So then you — if I understand — are *not* a Swedenborgian, ma'am?"

"If I were, I certainly should have had no inducement to join myself to your church," she replied, with gentle dignity. "I believe, with all my heart, in the same Bible and the same creed that you believe in, Deacon Quirk."

"And you *live* your creed, which all such genial Christians do not find it necessary to do," I thought, as the Deacon in some perplexity took his departure, and she returned with a smile to her sewing.

I suppose the call came about in this way. We had the sewing-circle here last week, and just before the lamps were lighted, and when people had dropped their work to group and talk in the corners, Meta Tripp came up with one or two other girls to Aunt Winifred, and begged "to hear some of those queer things people said she believed about heaven." Auntie is never obtrusive with her views on this or any other matter, but being thus urged, she answered a few questions that they put to her, to the extreme scandal of one or two old ladies, and the secret delight of the rest.

"Well," said little Mrs. Bland, squeezing and kissing her youngest, who was at that moment vigorously employed in sticking very long darning-needles into his mother's water-fall, "I hope there'll be a great many babies there. I should be perfectly happy if I always could have babies to play with!"

The look that Aunt Winifred shot over at me was worth seeing.

She merely replied, however, that she supposed all our "highest aspirations," — with an indescribable accent to which Mrs. Bland was safely deaf, — if good ones, would be realized; and added, laughing, that Swedenborg said that the babies in heaven — who outnumber the grown people — will be given into the charge of those women especially fond of them.

"Swedenborg is suggestive, even if you can't accept what

seem to the uninitiated to be his natural impossibilities," she said, after we had discussed Deacon Quirk awhile. "He says a pretty thing, too, occasionally. Did I ever read you about the houses?" She had not, and I wished to hear, so she found the book on Heaven and Hell, and read: —

"As often as I have spoken with the angels mouth to mouth, so often I have been with them in their habitations: their habitations are altogether like the habitations on earth which are called houses, but more beautiful; in them are parlors, rooms, and chambers in great numbers; there are also courts, and round about are gardens, shrubberies, and fields. Palaces of heaven have been seen which were so magnificent that they could not be described; above, they glittered as if they were of pure gold, and below, as if they were of precious stones; one palace was more splendid than another; within, it was the same; the rooms were ornamented with such decorations as neither words nor sciences are sufficient to describe. On the side which looked to the south there were paradises, where all things in like manner glittered, and in some places the leaves were as of silver, and the fruits as of gold; and the flowers on their beds presented by colors as it were rainbows; at the boundaries again were palaces, in which the view terminated."

Aunt Winifred says that our hymns, taken all together, contain the worst and the best pictures of heaven that we have in any branch of literature.

"It seems to me incredible," she says, "that the Christian Church should have allowed that beautiful 'Jerusalem' in its hymnology so long, with the ghastly couplet, —

'Where congregations ne'er break up,
And Sabbaths have no end.'

The dullest preachers are sure to give it out, and that when there are the greatest number of restless children wondering

when it will be time to go home. It is only within ten years
that modern hymn-books have altered it, returning in part to
the original.

"I do not think we have chosen the best parts of that hymn
for our 'service of song.' You never read the whole of it? You
don't know how pretty it is! It is a relief from the customary
palms and choirs. One's whole heart is glad of the outlet of its
sweet refrain, —

> 'Would God that I were there!'

before one has half read it. You are quite ready to believe that

> 'There is no hunger, heat, nor cold,
>   But *pleasure every way.*'

Listen to this: —

> 'Thy houses are of ivory,
>   Thy windows crystal clear,
> Thy tiles are made of beaten gold;
>   O God, that I were there!

> 'We that are here in banishment
>   Continually do moan.
>   .   .   .   .   .

> 'Our sweet is mixed with bitter gall,
>   Our pleasure is but pain,
> Our joys scarce last the looking on,
>   Our sorrows still remain.

> 'But there they live in such delight,
>   *Such pleasure and such play,*
> As that to them a thousand years
>   Doth seem as yesterday.'

And this: —

> 'Thy gardens and thy gallant walks
>   Continually are green;

There grow such sweet and pleasant flowers
As nowhere else are seen.

'There cinnamon, there sugar grows,
There nard and balm abound,
What tongue can tell, or heart conceive
The joys that there are found?

'Quite through the streets, with silver sound,
The flood of life doth flow,
Upon whose banks, on every side,
The wood of life doth grow.'

I tell you we may learn something from that grand old Catholic singer.[15] He is far nearer to the Bible than the innovators on his MSS. Do you not notice how like his images are to the inspired ones, and yet how pleasant and natural is the effect of the entire poem?

"There is nobody like Bonar, though, to sing about heaven.[16] There is one of his, 'We shall meet and rest,' — do you know it?

I shook my head, and knelt down beside her and watched her face, — it was quite unconscious of me, the musing face, — while she repeated dreamily: —

"Where the faded flower shall freshen, —
Freshen nevermore to fade;
Where the shaded sky shall brighten, —
Brighten nevermore to shade;
Where the sun-blaze never scorches;
Where the star-beams cease to chill;
Where no tempest stirs the echoes
Of the wood or wave or hill; . . . .
Where no shadow shall bewilder;
Where life's vain parade is o'er;

[15] "That grand old Catholic singer" evidently refers to St. Augustine, to whom the hymn "Jerusalem" was traditionally attributed.
[16] Horatius Bonar (1818-1889), a Scottish divine, wrote many hymns and religious poems.

Where the sleep of sin is broken,
    And the dreamer dreams no more;
Where the bond is never severed, —
    Partings, claspings, sob and moan,
Midnight waking, twilight weeping,
    Heavy noontide, — all are done;
Where the child has found its mother;
    Where the mother finds the child;
Where dear families are gathered,
    That were scattered on the wild; . . . .
Where the hidden wound is healed;
    Where the blighted life reblooms;
Where the smitten heart the freshness
    Of its buoyant youth resumes; . . . .
Where we find the joy of loving,
    As we never loved before, —
Loving on, unchilled, unhindered,
    Loving once, forevermore." . . . .

30th.

Aunt Winifred was weeding her day-lilies this morning, when the gate creaked timidly, and then swung noisily, and in walked Abinadab Quirk, with a bouquet of China pinks in the button-hole of his green-gray linen coat. He had taken evident pains to smarten himself up a little, for his hair was combed into two horizontal *dabs* over his ears, and the green-gray coat and blue-checked shirt-sleeves were quite clean; but he certainly is the most uncouth specimen of six feet five that it has ever been my privilege to behold. I feel sorry for him, though. I heard Meta Tripp laughing at him in Sunday school the other day, — "Quadrangular Quirk," she called him, a little too loud, and the poor fellow heard her. He half turned, blushing fiercely; then slunk down in his corner with as pitiable a look as is often seen upon a man's face.

He came up to Auntie awkwardly, — a part of the scene I saw from the window, and the rest she told me, — head hanging, and the tiny bouquet held out.

"Clo sent these to you," he stammered out, — "my cousin Clo. I was coming 'long, and she thought, you know, — she'd get me, you see, to — to — that is, to — bring them. She sent her — that is — let me see. She sent her respect — ful — respectful — no, her love; that was it. She sent her love 'long with 'em."

Mrs. Forceythe dropped her weeds, and held out her white, shapely hands, wet with the heavy dew, to take the flowers.

"O, thank you! Clo knows my fancy for pinks. How kind in you to bring them! Won't you sit down a few moments? I was just going to rest a little. Do you like flowers?"

Abinadab eyed the white hands, as his huge fingers just touched them, with a sort of awe; and, sighing, sat down on the very edge of the garden bench beside her. After a singular variety of efforts to take the most uncomfortable position of which he was capable, he succeeded to his satisfaction, and, growing then somewhat more at his ease, answered her question.

"Flowers are such *gassy* things. They just blow out and that's the end of 'em. *I* like machine-shops best."

"Ah! well, that is a very useful liking. Do you ever invent machinery yourself?"

"Sometimes," said Abinadab, with a bashful smile. "There's a little improvement of mine for carpet-sweepers up before the patent-office now. Don't know whether they 'll run it through. Some of the chaps I saw in Boston told me they thought they would do 't in time; it takes an awful sight of time. I'm alwers fussing over something of the kind; alwers did, sence I was a baby; had my little wind-mills and carts and things; used to sell 'em to the other young uns. Father don't like it. He wants me to stick to the farm. I don't like farming. I feel like a fish out of water. — Mrs. Forceythe, marm!"

He turned on her with an abrupt change of tone, so funny that she could with difficulty retain her gravity.

"I heard you saying a sight of queer things the other day

about heaven. Clo, she's been telling me a sight more. Now, *I* never believed in heaven!"

"Why?"

"Because I don't believe," said the poor fellow, with sullen decision, "that a benevolent God ever would ha' made sech a derned awkward chap as I am!"

Aunt Winifred replied by stepping into the house, and bringing out a fine photograph of one of the best of the St. Georges, — a rapt, yet very manly face, in which the saint and the hero are wonderfully blended. "I suppose," she said, putting it into his hands, "that if you should go to heaven, you would be as much fairer than that picture as that picture is fairer than you are now."

"No! Why, would I, though? Jim-miny! Why, it would be worth going for, would n't it?"

The words were no less reverently spoken than the vague rhapsodies of his father; for the sullenness left his face, and his eyes — which are pleasant, and not unmanly, when one fairly sees them — sparkled softly, like a child's.

"Make it all up there, maybe?" musing, — "the girls laughing at you all your life, and all? That would be the bigger heft of the two then, would n't it? for they say there ain't any end to things up there. Why, so it might be fair in Him after all; more 'n fair, perhaps. See here, Mrs. Forceythe, I 'm not a church-member, you know, and father, he's dreadful troubled about me; prays over me like a span of ministers, the old gentleman does, every Sunday night. Now, I don't want to go to the other place any more than the next man, and I've had my times, too, of thinking I'd keep steady and say my prayers reg'lar, — it makes a chap feel on a sight better terms with himself, — but I don't see how *I'm* going to wear white frocks and stand up in a choir, — never could sing no more'n a frog with a cold in his head, — it tires me more now, honest, to think of it, than it does to do a week's mowing. Look at me! Do you s'pose I'm fit for it? Father, he's always talking about the thrones, and the wings, and the praises, and the palms, and having new names in your foreheads (should n't object to that, though, by any means), till he drives me into the tool-house, or off on a spree. I tell him if God ain't got a place where chaps like me can do something He's fitted 'em to do in this world, there's no use thinking about it anyhow."

So Auntie took the honest fellow into her most earnest thought for half an hour, and argued, and suggested, and re-proved, and helped him, as only she could do; and at the end of it seemed to have worked into his mind some distinct and not unwelcome ideas of what a Christ-like life must mean to him, and of the coming heaven which is so much more real to her than any life outside of it.

"And then," she told him, "I imagine that your fancy for machinery will be employed in some way. Perhaps you will do a great deal more successful inventing there than you ever will here."

"You don't say so!" said radiant Abinadab.

"God will give you something to do, certainly, and some-thing that you will like."

"I might turn it to some religious purpose, you know!" said Abinadab, looking bright. "Perhaps I could help 'em build a church, or hist some of their pearl gates, or something like!"

Upon that he said that it was time to be at home and see to the oxen, and shambled awkwardly away.

Clo told us this afternoon that he begged the errand and the flowers from her. She says: " 'Bin thinks there never was any-body like you, Mrs. Forceythe, and 'Bin is n't the only one, either." At which Mrs. Forceythe smiles absently, thinking — I wonder of what.

Monday night.

I saw as funny and as pretty a bit of drama this afternoon as I have seen for a long time.

Faith had been rolling out in the hot hay ever since three o'clock, with one of the little Blands, and when the shadows grew long they came in with flushed cheeks and tumbled hair, to rest and cool upon the door-steps. I was sitting in the parlor, sewing energetically on some sun-bonnets for some of Aunt Winifred's people down town, — I found the heat to be more bearable if I kept busy, — and could see, unseen, all the little *tableaux* into which the two children grouped themselves; a new one every instant; in the shadow now, — now in a quiver of golden glow; the wind tossing their hair about, and their chatter chiming down the hall like bells.

"O, what a funny little sunset there's going to be behind the maple-tree," said the blond-haired Bland, in a pause.

"Funny enough," observed Faith, with her superior smile, "but it's going to be a great deal funnier up in heaven, I tell you, Molly Bland."

"Funny in heaven? Why, Faith!" Molly drew herself up with a religious air, and looked the image of her father.

"Yes, to be sure. I'm going to have some little pink blocks made out of it when I go; pink and yellow and green and purple and — O, so many blocks! I'm going to have a little red cloud to sail round in, like that one up over the house, too, I should n't wonder."

Molly opened her eyes. "O, I don't believe it."

"*You* don't know much!" said Miss Faith, superbly. "I should n't s'pose you would believe it. P'r'aps I'll have some strawberries too, and some ginger-snaps, — I'm not going to have any old bread and butter up there, — O, and some little gold apples, and a lot of playthings; nicer playthings — why, nicer than they have in the shops in Boston, Molly Bland! God's keeping 'em up there a purpose."

"Dear me!" said incredulous Molly, "I should just like to know who told you that much. My mother never told it at me. Did your mother tell it at you?"

"O, she told me some of it, and the rest I thinked out my-self."

"Let's go and play One Old Cat," said Molly, with an un-comfortable jump; "I wish I had n't got to go to heaven!"

"Why, Molly Bland! why, I think heaven's splendid! I've got my papa up there, you know. 'Here's my little girl!' That's what he's going to say. Mamma, she'll be there, too, and we're all going to live in the prettiest house. I have dreadful hurries to go this afternoon sometimes when Phoebe's cross and won't give me sugar. They don't let you in, though, 'nless you're a good girl."

"Who gets it all up?" asked puzzled Molly.

"Jesus Christ will give me all these beautiful fings," said Faith, evidently repeating her mother's words, — the only catechism that she has been taught.

"And what will He do when He sees you?" asked her mother, coming down the stairs and stepping up behind her.

"Take me up in His arms and kiss me."

"And what will Faith say?"

"*Fank — you!*" said the child, softly.

In another minute she was absorbed, body and soul, in the mysteries of One Old Cat.

"But I don't think she will feel much like being naughty for half an hour to come," her mother said; "hear how pleasantly her words drop! Such a talk quiets her, like a hand laid on her head. Mary, sometimes I think it is His very hand, as much as when He touched those other little children. I wish Faith to feel at home with Him and His home. Little thing! I really do not think that she is conscious of any fear of dying; I do not think it means anything to her but Christ, and her father, and pink blocks, and a nice time, and never disobeying me or be-ing cross. Many a time she wakes me up in the morning talk-ing away to herself, and when I turn and look at her, she says:

'O mamma, won't we go to heaven to-day, you fink? *When* will we go, mamma?'"

"If there had been any pink blocks and ginger-snaps for me when I was at her age, I should not have prayed every night to 'die out.' I think the horrors of death that children live through, unguessed and unrelieved, are awful. Faith may thank you all her life that she has escaped them."

"I should feel answerable to God for the child's soul, if I had not prevented that. I always wanted to know what sort of mother that poor little thing had, who asked, if she were *very* good up in heaven, whether they would n't let her go down to hell Saturday afternoons, and play a little while!"

"I know. But think of it, — blocks and ginger-snaps!"

"I treat Faith just as the Bible treats us, by dealing in *pictures* of truth that she can understand. I can make Clo and Abinadab Quirk comprehend that their pianos and machinery may not be made of literal rosewood and steel, but will be some synonyme of the thing, which will answer just such wants of their changed natures as rosewood and steel must answer now. There will be machinery and pianos in the same sense in which there will be pearl gates and harps. Whatever enjoyment any or all of them represent now, something will represent then.

"But Faith, if I told her that her heavenly ginger-snaps would not be made of molasses and flour, would have a cry, for fear that she was not going to have any ginger-snaps at all; so, until she is older, I give her unqualified ginger-snaps. The principal joy of a child's life consists in eating. Faith begins, as soon as the light wanes, to dream of that gum-drop which she is to have at bedtime. I don't suppose she can outgrow that at once by passing out of her little round body. She must begin where she left off, — nothing but a baby, though it will be as holy and happy a baby as Christ can make it.

When she says: 'Mamma, I shall be hungery and want my dinner, up there,' I never hesitate to tell her that she shall have her dinner. She would never, in her secret heart, though she might not have the honesty to say so, expect to be otherwise than miserable in a dinnerless eternity."

"You are not afraid of misleading the child's fancy?"

"Not so long as I can keep the two ideas — that Christ is her best friend, and that heaven is not meant for naughty girls — pre-eminent in her mind. And I sincerely believe that He would give her the very pink blocks which she anticipates, no less than He would give back a poet his lost dreams, or you your brother. He has been a child; perhaps, incidentally to the unsolved mysteries of atonement, for this very reason, — that He may know how to 'prepare their places' for them, whose angels do always behold His Father. Ah, you may be sure that, if of such is the happy Kingdom, He will not scorn to stoop and fit it to their little needs.

"There was that poor little fellow whose guineapig died, — do you remember?"

"Only half; what was it?"

" 'O mamma,' he sobbed out, behind his handkerchief, 'don't great big elephants have souls?'

" 'No, my son.'

" 'Nor camels, mamma?'

" 'No.'

" 'Nor bears, nor alligators, nor chickens?'

" 'O no, dear.'

" 'O mamma, mamma! Don't little CLEAN — *white* — *guinea-pigs* have souls?'

"I never should have had the heart to say no to that; especially as we have no positive proof to the contrary.

"Then that scrap of a boy who lost his little red balloon the morning he bought it, and, broken-hearted, wanted to know whether it had gone to heaven. Don't I suppose if he had been

taken there himself that very minute, that he would have
found a little balloon in waiting for him? How can I help it?"

"It has a pretty sound. If people would not think it so material and shocking — "

"Let people read Martin Luther's letter to his little boy.
There is the testimony of a pillar in good and regular standing!
I don't think you need be afraid of my balloon after that."

I remembered that there was a letter of his on heaven, but,
not recalling it distinctly, I hunted for it to-night, and read it
over. I shall copy it, the better to retain it in mind.[17]

"Grace and peace in Christ, my dear little son. I see with
pleasure that thou learnest well, and prayed diligently. Do so,
my son, and continue. When I come home I will bring thee a
pretty fairing.

"I know a pretty, merry garden wherein are many children.
They have little golden coats, and they gather beautiful apples
under the trees, and pears, cherries, plums, and wheat-plums;
— they sing, and jump, and are merry. They have beautiful
little horses, too, with gold bits and silver saddles. And I asked
the man to whom the garden belongs, whose children they
were. And he said: 'They are the children that love to pray
and to learn, and are good.' Then said I: 'Dear man, I have a
son, too; his name is Johnny Luther. May he not also come
into this garden and eat these beautiful apples and pears, and
ride these fine horses?' Then the man said: 'If he loves to pray
and to learn, and is good, he shall come into this garden, and
Lippus and Jost too; and when they all come together, they
shall have fifes and trumpets, lutes and all sorts of music, and
they shall dance, and shoot with little cross-bows.'

"And he showed me a fine meadow there in the garden,
made for dancing. There hung nothing but golden fifes,

[17] Elizabeth Stuart Phelps found this letter in Mrs. Charles's *Chronicles
of the Schönberg-Cotta Family*, but in "copying" it she made the pleasures
of heaven more concrete and the language even more colloquial.

trumpets, and fine silver cross-bows. But it was early, and the children had not yet eaten; therefore I could not wait the dance, and I said to the man: 'Ah, dear sir! I will immediately go and write all this to my little son Johnny, and tell him to pray diligently, and to learn well, and to be good, so that he also may come to this garden. But he has an Aunt Lehne, he must bring her with him.' Then the man said: 'It shall be so; go, and write him so.'

"Therefore, my dear little son Johnny, learn and pray away! and tell Lippus and Jost, too, that they must learn and pray. And then you shall come to the garden together. Herewith I commend thee to Almighty God. And greet Aunt Lehne, and give her a kiss for my sake.

"Thy dear Father,
"MARTINUS LUTHER.

"ANNO 1530."

◂• XIII •▸

THE summer is sliding quietly away, — my desolate summer
which I dreaded; with the dreams gone from its wild-flowers,
the crown from its sunsets, the thrill from its winds and its
singing.

But I have found out a thing. One can live without dreams
and crowns and thrills.

I have not lost them. They lie under the ivied cross with
Roy for a little while. They will come back to me with him.
"Nothing is lost," she teaches me. And until they come back,
I see — for she shows me — fields groaning under their white
harvest, with laborers very few. Ruth followed the sturdy
reapers, gleaning a little. I, perhaps, can do as much. The ways
in which I must work seem so small and insignificant, so pitifully trivial sometimes, that I do not even like to write them
down here. In fact, they are so small that, six months ago, I
did not see them at all. Only to be pleasant to old Phoebe,
and charitable to Meta Tripp, and faithful to my *not* very interesting little scholars, and a bit watchful of worn-out Mrs.
Bland, and — But dear me, I won't! They *are* so little!

But one's self becomes of less importance, which seems to
be the point.

It seems very strange to me sometimes, looking back to
those desperate winter days, what a change has come over my

thoughts of Roy. Not that he is any less — O, never any less to me. But it is almost as if she had raised him from the grave. Why seek ye the living among the dead? Her soft, compassionate eyes shine with the question every hour. And every hour he is helping me, — ah, Roy, we understand one another now.

How he must love Aunt Winifred! How pleasant the days will be when we can talk her over, and thank her together!

"To be happy because Roy is happy." I remember how those first words of hers struck me. It does not seem to me impossible, now.

Aunt Winifred and I laugh at each other for talking so much about heaven. I see that the green book is filled with my questions and her answers. The fact is, not that we do not talk as much about mundane affairs as other people, but that this one thing interests us more.

If, instead, it had been flounces, or babies, or German philosophy, the green book would have filled itself just as unconsciously with flounces, or babies, or German philosophy. This interest in heaven is of course no sign of especial piety in me, nor could people with young, warm, uncrushed hopes throbbing through their days be expected to feel the same. It is only the old principle of where the treasure is — the heart.

"How spiritual-minded Mary has grown!" Mrs. Bland observes, regarding me respectfully. I try in vain to laugh her out of the conviction. If Roy had not gone before, I should think no more, probably, about the coming life, than does the minister's wife herself.

But now — I cannot help it — that is the reality, this the dream; that the substance, this the shadow.

The other day Aunt Winifred and I had a talk which has been of more value to me than all the rest. Faith was in bed; it was a cold, rainy evening; we were secure from callers; we lighted a few kindlers in the parlor grate; she rolled up the easy-chair, and I took my cricket at her feet.

"Paul at the feet of Gamaliel! This is what I call comfort. Now, Auntie, let us go to heaven awhile."

"Very well. What do you want there now?"

I paused a moment, sobered by a thought that has been growing steadily upon me of late.

"Something more, Aunt Winifred. All these other things are beautiful and dear; but I believe I want — God.

"You have not said much about Him. The Bible says a great deal about Him. You have given me the filling-up of heaven in all its pleasant promise, but — I don't know — there seems to be an outline wanting."

She drew my hand up into hers, smiling.

"I have not done my painting by artistic methods, I know; but it was not exactly accidental.

"Tell me, honestly, — is God more to you or less, a more distinct Being or a more vague one, than He was six months ago? Is He, or is He not, dearer to you now than then?"

I thought about it a minute, and then turned my face up to her.

"Mary, what a light in your eyes! How is it?"

It came over me slowly, but it came with such a passion of gratitude and unworthiness, that I scarcely knew how to tell her — that He never has been to me, in all my life, what He is now at the end of these six months. He was once an abstract Grandeur which I struggled more in fear than love to please. He has become a living Presence, dear and real.

> "No dead fact stranded on the shore
>   Of the oblivious years;
>   But warm, sweet, tender, even yet
>   A present help." . . . .

He was an inexorable Mystery who took Roy from me to lose him in the glare of a more inexorable heaven. He is a

Father who knew better than we that we should be parted
for a while; but He only means it to be a little while. He is
keeping him for me to find in the flush of some summer morning, on which I shall open my eyes no less naturally than I
open them on June sunrises now. I always have that fancy of
going in the morning.

She understood what I could not tell her, and said, "I
thought it would be so."

"You, His interpreter, have done it," I answered her. "His
heaven shows what he is, — don't you see? — like a friend's
letter. I could no more go back to my old groping relations to
Him, than I could make of you the dim and somewhat apoc-
ryphal Western Auntie that you were before I saw you."

"Which was precisely why I have dealt with this subject as
I have," she said. "You had all your life been directed to an
indefinite heaven, where the glory of God was to crowd out
all individuality and all human joy from His most individual
and human creatures, till the 'Glory of God' had become nothing but a name and a dread to you. So I let those three words
slide by, and tried to bring you to them, as Christ brought the
Twelve to believe in him, 'for the works' sake.'

"Yes, my child; clinging human loves, stifled longings, cries
for rest, forgotten hopes, shall have their answer. Whatever
the bewilderment of beauties folded away for us in heavenly
nature and art, they shall strive with each other to make us
glad. These things have their pleasant place. But, through
eternity, there will be always something beyond and dearer
than the dearest of them. God himself will be first, — naturally
and of necessity, without strain or struggle, *first*."

When I sat here last winter with my dead in my house,
those words would have roused in me an agony of wild
questionings. I should have beaten about them and beaten
against them, and cried in my honest heart that they were
false. I *knew* that I loved Roy more than I loved such a Being
as God seemed to me then to be. Now, they strike me as

simply and pleasantly true. The more I love Roy, the more I love Him. He loves us both.

"You see it could not be otherwise," she went on, speaking low. "Where would you be, or I, or they who seem to us so much dearer and better than ourselves, if it were not for Jesus Christ? What can heaven be to us, but a song of the love that is the same to us yesterday, to-day, and forever, — that, in the mystery of an intensity which we shall perhaps never understand, could choose death and be glad in the choosing, and, what is more than that, could live *life* for us for three-and-thirty years?

"I cannot strain my faith — or rather my common sense — to the rhapsodies with which many people fill heaven. But it seems to me like this: A friend goes away from us, and it may be seas or worlds that lie between us, and we love him. He leaves behind him his little keepsakes; a lock of hair to curl about our fingers; a picture that has caught the trick of his eyes or smile; a book, a flower, a letter. What we do with the curling hair, what we say to the picture, what we dream over the flower and the letter, nobody knows but ourselves. People have risked life for such mementos. Yet who loves the senseless gift more than the giver, — the curl more than the young forehead on which it fell, — the letter more than the hand which traced it?

"So it seems to me that we shall learn to see in God the centre of all possibilities of joy. The greatest of these lesser delights is but the greater measure of His friendship. They will not mean less of pleasure, but more of Him. They will not 'pale,' as Dr. Bland would say. Human dearness will wax, not wane, in heaven; but human friends will be loved for love of him."

"I see; that helps me; like a torch in a dark room. But there will be shadows in the corners. Do you suppose that we shall ever *fully* feel it in the body?"

"In the body, probably not. We see through a glass so

darkly that the temptation to idolatry is always our greatest.
Golden images did not die with Paganism. At times I fancy
that, somewhere between this world and another, a revelation
will come upon us like a flash, of what *sin* really is, — such
a revelation, lighting up the lurid background of our past in
such colors, that the consciousness of what Christ has done
for us will be for a time as much as heart can bear. After
that, the mystery will be, not how to love Him most, but
that we ever *could* have loved any creature or thing as much."

"We serve God quite as much by active work as by special
prayer, here," I said after some thought; "how will it be
there?"

"We must be busily at work certainly; but I think there
must naturally be more communion with Him then. Now,
this phrase 'communion with God' has been worn, and not
always well worn.

"Prayer means to us, in this life, more often penitent con-
fession than happy interchange of thought with Him. It is
associated, too, with aching limbs and sleepy eyes, and nights
when the lamp goes out. Obstacles, moral and physical, stand
in the way of our knowing exactly what it may mean in the
ideal of it.

"My best conception of it lies in the *friendship* of the man
Christ Jesus. I suppose he will bear with him, eternally, the
humanity which he took up with him from the Judean hills.
I imagine that we shall see him in visible form like ourselves,
among us, yet not of us; that he, himself, is "Gott mit ihnen";
that we shall talk with him as a man talketh with his friend.
Perhaps, bowed and hushed at his dear feet, we shall hear
from his own lips the story of Nazareth, of Bethany, of Gol-
gotha, of the chilly mountains where he used to pray all night
long for us; of the desert places where he hungered; of his
cry for help — think, Mary — *His!* — when there was not
one in all the world to hear it, and there was silence in heaven,

while angels strengthened him and man forsook him. Perhaps his voice — the very voice which has sounded whispering through our troubled life — "Could ye not watch one hour?" — shall unfold its perplexed meanings; shall make its rough places plain; shall show us step by step the merciful way by which he led us to that hour; shall point out to us, joy by joy, the surprises that he has been planning for us, just as the old father in the story planned to surprise his wayward boy come home.

"And such a 'communion,' — which is not too much, nor yet enough, to dare to expect of a God who was the 'friend' of Abraham, who 'walked' with Enoch, who did not call fishermen his servants, — *such* will be that 'presence of God,' that 'adoration,' on which we have looked from afar off with despairing eyes that wept, they were so dazzled, and turned themselves away as from the thing they greatly feared."

I think we neither of us cared to talk for a while after this. Something made me forget even that I was going to see Roy in heaven. "Three-and-thirty years. Three-and-thirty years." The words rang themselves over.

"It is on the humanity of Christ, she said after some musing, "that all my other reasons for hoping for such a heaven as I hope for rest for foundation. He knows exactly what we are, for he has been one of us; exactly what we hope and fear and crave, for he has hoped and feared and craved, not the less humanly, but only more intensely.

" '*If it were not so,*' — do you take in the thoughtful tenderness of that? A mother stilling her frightened child in the dark, might speak just so, — '*if it were not so, I would have told you.*' That brooding love makes room for all that we can want. He has sounded every deep of a troubled and tempted life. Who so sure as he to understand how to prepare a place where troubled and tempted lives may grow serene? Further than this; since he stands as our great Type, no less in death and after than before it, he answers for us many of these lesser questions on the event of which so much of our happiness depends.

"Shall we lose our personality in a vague ocean of ether, — you one puff of gas, I another? —

"He, with his own wounded body, rose and ate and walked and talked.

"Is all memory of this life to be swept away? —

"He, arisen, has forgotten nothing. He waits to meet his disciples at the old, familiar places; as naturally as if he had never been parted from them, he falls in with the current of their thoughts.

"Has any one troubled us with fears that in the glorified crowds of heaven we may miss a face dearer than all the world to us? —

"He made himself known to his friends, — Mary and the two at Emmaus, and the bewildered group praying and perplexed in their bolted room.

"Do we weary ourselves with speculations whether human loves can outlive the shock of death? —

"Mary knew how He loved her, when, turning, she heard him call her by her name. They knew, whose hearts 'burned within them while he talked with them by the way, and when he tarried with them, the day being far spent.' "

"And for the rest?"

"For the rest, about which He was silent, we can trust him, and if, trusting, we please ourselves with fancies, he would be the last to think it blame to us. There is one promise which grows upon me the more I study it, 'He that spared not his own Son, how shall he not also *with him freely give us all things?*' Sometimes I wonder if that does not infold a beautiful *double entendre*, a hint of much that you and I have conjectured, — as one throws down a hint of a surprise to a child.

"Then there is that pledge to those who seek first His kingdom: '*All these things shall be added unto you.*' 'These things,' were food and clothing, were varieties of material delight, and the words were spoken to men who lived hungry, beggared, and died the death of outcasts. If this passage could be taken literally, it would be very significant in its bearing on the future life; for Christ must keep his promise to the letter, in one world or another. It may be wrenching the verse, not as a verse, but from the grain of the argument, to insist on the literal interpretation, — though I am not sure."

⊷ XIV ⊷

I ASKED the other day, wondering whether all ministers were like Dr. Bland, what Uncle Forceythe used to believe about heaven.

"Very much what I do," she said. "These questions were brought home to him, early in life, by the death of a very dear sister; he had thought much about them. I think one of the things that so much attached his people to him was the way he had of weaving their future life in with this, till it grew naturally and pleasantly into their frequent thought. O yes, your uncle supplied me with half of my proof-texts."

Aunt Winifred has not looked quite well of late, I fancy; though it may be only fancy. She has not spoken of it, except one day when I told her that she looked pale. It was the heat, she said.

20th.

Little Clo came over to-night. I believe she thinks Aunt Winifred the best friend she has in the world. Auntie has become much attached to all her scholars, and has a rare power of winning her way into their confidence. They come to her with all their little interests, — everything, from saving their souls to trimming a bonnet. Clo, however, is the favorite, as I predicted.

She looked a bit blue to-night, as girls will look; in fact, her face always has a tinge of sadness about it. Aunt Winifred, understanding at a glance that the child was not in a mood to talk before a third, led her away into the garden, and they were gone a long time. When it grew dark, I saw them coming up the path, Clo's hand locked in her teacher's, and her face, which was wet, upturned like a child's. They strolled to the gate, lingered a little to talk, and then Clo said good night without coming in.

Auntie sat for a while after she had gone, thinking her over, I could see. "Poor thing!" she said at last, half to herself, half to me, — "poor little foolish thing! This is where the dreadful individuality of a human soul irks me. There comes a point, beyond which you *can't* help people."

"What has happened to Clo?"

"Nothing, lately. It has been happening for two years. Two miserable years are an eternity, at Clo's age. It is the old story, — a summer boarder; a little flirting; a little dreaming; a little pain; then autumn, and the nuts dropping on the leaves, and he was gone, — and knew not what he did, — and the child waked up. There was the future; to bake and sweep, to go to sewing-circles, and sing in the choir, and bear the moonlight nights, — and she loved him. She has lived through two years of it, and she loves him now. Reason will not reach such a passion in a girl like Clo. I did not tell her that she would put it away with other girlish things, and laugh at it herself some happy day, as women have laughed at their young fancies before her; partly because that would be a certain way of repelling her confidence, — she does not believe it, and my believing could not make her; partly because I am not quite sure about it myself. Clo has a good deal of the woman about her; her introspective life is intense. She may cherish this sweet misery as she does her musical tastes, till it has struck deep root. There is nothing in the excellent Mrs. Bentley's household, nor in Homer anywhere, to draw the girl out from herself in time to prevent the dream from becoming a reality."

"Poor little thing! What did you say to her?"

"You ought to have heard what she said to me! I wish I were at liberty to tell you the whole story. What troubles her most is that it is not going to help the matter any to die. 'O Mrs. Forceythe,' she says, in a tone that is enough to give the hearteache, even to such an old woman as Mrs. Forceythe, 'O Mrs. Forceythe, what is going to become of me up there? He never loved me, you see, and he never, never will, and he will have some beautiful, good wife of his own, and I won't have *any*body! For I can't love anybody else, — I've tried; I tried just as hard as I could to love my cousin 'Bin; he's real good, and — I'm — afraid 'Bin likes me, though I guess he likes his carpet-sweepers better. O, sometimes I think, and think, till it seems as if I could not bear it! I don't see how God can *make* me happy. I wish I could be buried up and go to sleep, and never have any heaven!' "

"And you told her — ?"

"That she should have him there. That is, if not himself, something, — somebody who would so much more than fill his place, that she would never have a lonely or unloved minute. Her eyes brightened, and shaded, and pondered, doubting. She 'did n't see how it could ever be.' I told her not to try and see how, but to leave it to Christ. He knew all about this little trouble of hers, and he would make it right.

" 'Will he?' she questioned, sighing; 'but there are so many of us! There's 'Bin, and a plenty more, and I don't see how it's going to be smoothed out. Everything is in a jumble, Mrs. Forceythe, don't you see? for some people *can't* like and keep liking so many times.' Something came into my mind about the rough places that shall be made plain, and the crooked things straight. I tried to explain to her, and at last I kissed away her tears, and sent her home, if not exactly comforted, a little less miserable, I think, than when she came. Ah, well, — I wonder myself sometimes about these 'crooked things'; but still I never doubt."

She finished her sentence somewhat hurriedly, and half started from her chair, raising both hands with a quick, involuntary motion that attracted my notice. The lights came in just then, and, unless I am much mistaken, her face showed paler than usual; but when I asked her if she felt faint, she said, 'O no, I believe I am a little tired, and will go to bed."

September 1.

I am glad that the summer is over. This heat has certainly worn on Aunt Winifred, with that kind of wear which slides people into confirmed invalidism. I suppose she would bear it in her saintly way, as she bears everything, but it would be a bitter cup for her. I know she was always pale, but this is a paleness which —

Night.

A dreadful thing has happened!

I was in the middle of my sentence, when I heard a commotion in the street, and a child's voice shouting incoherently something about the doctor, and *"mother's killed! O, mother's killed! mother's burnt to death!"* I was at the window in time to see a blond-haired girl running wildly past the house, and to see that it was Molly Bland.

At the same moment I saw Aunt Winifred snatching her hat from its nail in the entry. She beckoned to me to follow, and we were half-way over to the parsonage before I had a distinct thought of what I was about.

We came upon a horrible scene. Dr. Bland was trying to do everything alone; there was not a woman in the house to help him, for they have never been able to keep a servant, and none of the neighbors had had time to be there before us. The poor husband was growing faint, I think. Aunt Winifred saw by a look that he could not bear much more, sent him after Molly for the doctor, and took everything meantime into her own charge.

I shall not write down a word of it. It was a sight that, once seen, will never leave me as long as I live. My nerves are thoroughly shaken by it, and it must be put out of thought as far as possible.

It seems that the little boy — the baby — crept into the kitchen by himself, and began to throw the contents of the match-box on the stove, "to make a bonfire," the poor little fellow said. In five minutes his apron was ablaze. His mother was on the spot at his first cry, and smothered the little apron, and saved the child, but her dress was muslin, and everybody was too far off to hear her at first, — and by the time her husband came in from the garden it was too late.

She is living yet. Her husband, pacing the room back and forth, and crouching on his knees by the hour, is praying God to let her die before the morning.

Morning.

There is no chance of life, the doctor says. But he has been able to find something that has lessened her sufferings. She lies partially unconscious.

Wednesday night.

Aunt Winifred and I were over to the parsonage to-night, when she roused a little from her stupor and recognized us. She spoke to her husband, and kissed me good by, and asked for the children. They were playing softly in the next room; we sent for them, and they came in, — the four unconscious, motherless little things, — with the sunlight in their hair.

The bitterness of death came into her marred face at sight

of them, and she raised her hands to Auntie — to the only other mother there — with a sudden helpless cry: "I could bear it, I could bear it, if it were n't for *them*. Without any mother all their lives, — such little things, — and to go away where I can't do a single *thing* for them!"

Aunt Winifred stooped down and spoke low, but decidedly.

"You *will* do for them. God knows all about it. He will not send you away from them. You shall be just as much their mother, every day of their lives, as you have been here. Perhaps there is something to do for them which you never could have done here. He sees. He loves them. He loves you."

If I could paint, I might paint the look that struck through and through that woman's dying face; but words cannot touch it. If I were Aunt Winifred, I should bless God on my knees to-night for having shown me how to give such ease to a soul in death.

Thursday morning.

God is merciful. Mrs. Bland died at five o'clock.

10th.

How such a voice from the heavens shocks one out of the repose of calm sorrows and of calm joys. This has come and gone so suddenly that I cannot adjust it to any quiet and trustful thinking yet.

The whole parish mourns excitedly; for, though they worked their minister's wife hard, they loved her well. I cannot talk it over with the rest. It jars. Horror should never be dissected. Besides, my heart is too full of those four little children with the sunlight in their hair and the unconsciousness in their eyes.

15th.

Mrs. Quirk came over to-day in great perplexity. She had just come from the minister's.

"I don't know what we're a goin' to do with him!" she exclaimed in a gush of impatient, uncomprehending sympathy; "you can't let a man take on that way much longer. He'll worry himself sick, and then we shall either lose him or have to pay his bills to Europe! Why, he jest stops in the house, and walks his study up and down, day and night; or else he jest sets and sets and don't notice nobody but the children. Now I've jest ben over makin' him some chicken-pie, — he used to set a sight by my chicken-pie, — and he made believe to eat it, 'cause I'd ben at the trouble, I suppose, but how much do you suppose he swallowed? Jest three mouthfuls! Thinks says I, I won't spend my time over chicken-pie for the afflicted agin, and on ironing-day, too! When I knocked at the study door, he said 'Come in,' and stopped his walkin' and turned as quick.

" 'O,' says he, 'good morning. I thought it was Mrs. Forceythe.'

"I told him no, I was n't Mrs. Forceythe, but I'd come to comfort him in his sorrer all the same. But that's the only thing I have agin our minister. He won't *be* comforted. Mary Ann Jacobs, who's been there kind of looking after the children and things for him, you know, sence the funeral — she says he's asked three or four times for you, Mrs. Forceythe. There's ben plenty of his people in to see him, but you have n't ben nigh him, Mary Ann says."

"I stayed away because I thought the presence of friends at this time would be an intrusion," Auntie said; "but if he would like to see me, that alters the case; I will go, certainly."

"I don't know," suggested Mrs. Quirk, looking over the top of her spectacles, — I s'pose it's proper enough, but you bein' a widow, you know, and his wife — "

Aunt Winifred's eyes shot fire. She stood up and turned upon Mrs. Quirk with a look the like of which I presume

that worthy lady had never seen before, and is not likely to
see soon again (it gave the beautiful scorn of a Zenobia to
her fair, slight face), moved her lips slightly, but said nothing,
put on her bonnet, and went straight to Dr. Bland's.

The minister, they told her, was in his study. She knocked
lightly at the door, and was bidden in a lifeless voice to enter.

Shades and blinds were drawn, and the glare of the sun
quite shut out. Dr. Bland sat by his study-table, with his face
upon his hands. A Bible lay open before him. It had been lately
used; the leaves were wet.

He raised his head dejectedly, but smiled when he saw
who it was. He had been thinking about her, he said, and
was glad that she had come.

I do not know all that passed between them, but I gather,
from such hints as Auntie in her unconsciousness throws out,
that she had things to say which touched some comfortless
places in the man's heart. No Greek and Hebrew "original,"
no polished dogma, no link in his stereotyped logic, not one
of his eloquent sermons on the future state, came to his relief.

These were meant for happy days. They rang cold as steel
upon the warm needs of an afflicted man. Brought face to
face, and sharply, with the blank heaven of his belief, he
stood up from before his dead, and groped about it, and cried
out against it in the bitterness of his soul.

"I had no chance to prepare myself to bow to the will of
God," he said, his reserved ministerial manner in curious contrast with the caged way in which he was pacing the room,
— "I had no chance. I am taken by surprise, as by a thief in
the night. I had a great deal to say to her, and there was no
time. She could tell me what to do with my poor little children. I wanted to tell her other things. I wanted to tell her —
Perhaps we all of us have our regrets when the Lord removes
our friends; we may have done or left undone many things; we

might have made them happier. My mind does not rest with
assurance in its conceptions of the heavenly state. If I never
can tell her — "

He stopped abruptly, and paced into the darkest shadows
of the shadowed room, his face turned away.

"You said once some pleasant things about heaven?" he
said at last, half appealingly, stopping in front of her, hesitating; like a man and like a minister, hardly ready to come
with all the learning of his schools and commentators and sit
at the feet of a woman.

She talked with him for a time in her unobtrusive way, de-
ferring, when she honestly could, to his clerical judgment,
and careful not to wound him by any word; but frankly and
clearly, as she always talks.

When she rose to go he thanked her quietly.

"This is a somewhat novel train of thought to me," he
said; "I hope it may not prove an unscriptural one. I have been
reading the Book of Revelation to-day with these questions
especially in mind. We are never too old to learn. Some passages may be capable of other interpretations than I have
formerly given them. No matter what I *wish*, you see, I must
be guided by the Word of my God."

Auntie says that she never respected the man so much as
she did when, hearing those words, she looked up into his
haggard face, convulsed with its human pain and longing.

"I hope you do not think that *I* am not guided by the Word
of God," she answered. "I mean to be."

"I know you mean to be," he said cordially. "I do not say
that you are not. I may come to see that you are, and that
you are right. It will be a peaceful day for me if I can ever
quite agree with your methods of reasoning. But I must think
these things over. I thank you once more for coming. Your
sympathy is grateful to me."

Just as she closed the door he called her back.

"See," he said, with a saddened smile. "At least I shall never preach *this* again. It seems to me that life is always undoing for us something that we have just laboriously done."

He held up before her a mass of old blue manuscript, and threw it, as he spoke, upon the embers left in his grate. It smoked and blazed up and burned out.

It was that sermon on heaven of which there is an abstract in this journal.

20th.

Aunt Winifred hired Mr. Tripp's gray this afternoon, and drove to East Homer on some unexplained errand. She did not invite me to go with her, and Faith, though she teased impressively, was left at home. Her mother was gone till late, — so late that I had begun to be anxious about her, and heard through the dark the first sound of the buggy wheels with great relief. She looked very tired when I met her at the gate. She had not been able, she said, to accomplish her errand at East Homer, and from there had gone to Worcester by railroad, leaving Old Gray at the East Homer Eagle till her return. She told me nothing more, and I asked no questions.

⊸ XV ⊶

Faith has behaved like a witch all day. She knocked down three crickets and six hymn-books in church this morning, and this afternoon horrified the assembled and devout congregation by turning round in the middle of the long prayer, and, in a loud and distinct voice, asking Mrs. Quirk, for " 'nother those pepp'mints such as you gave me one Sunday a good many years ago, you 'member." After church, her mother tried a few Bible questions to keep her still.

"Faith, who was Christ's father?"

"Jerusalem!" said Faith, promptly.

"Where did his parents take Jesus when they fled from Herod?"

"O, to Europe. Of course I knew that! Everybody goes to Europe."

To-night when her mother had put her to bed, she came down laughing.

"Faith does seem to have a hard time with the Lord's Prayer. To-night, being very sleepy and in a hurry to finish, she proceeded with great solemnity: — 'Our Father who art in heaven, hallowed be thy name; six days shalt thou labor and do all thy work, and — Oh!'

"I was just thinking how amused her father must be."

Auntie says many such things. I cannot explain how pleasantly they strike me, nor how they help me.

Dr. Bland gave us a good sermon yesterday. There is an indescribable change in all his sermons. There is a change, too, in the man, and that something more than the haggardness of grief. I not only respect him and am sorry for him, but I feel more ready to be taught by him than ever before. A certain indefinable *humanness* softens his eyes and tones, and seems to be creeping into everything that he says. Yet, on the other hand, his people say that they have never heard him speak such pleasant, helpful things concerning his and their relations to God. I met him the other night, coming away from his wife's grave, and was struck by the expression of his face. I wondered if he were not slowly finding the "peaceful day," of which he told Aunt Winifred.

She, by the way, has taken another of her mysterious trips to Worcester.

30th.

We were wondering to-day where it will be, — I mean heaven.

"It is impossible to do more than wonder," Auntie said, "though we are explicitly told that there will be new heavens *and* a new earth, which seems, if anything can be taken literally in the Bible, to point to this world as the future home of at least some of us."

"Not for all of us, of course?"

"I don't feel sure. I know that somebody spent his valuable time in estimating that all the people who have lived and died upon the earth would cover it, alive or buried, twice over; but I know that somebody else claims with equal solemnity to have discovered that they could all be buried in the State of Pennsylvania! But it would be of little consequence if we could not all find room here, since there must be other provision for us."

"Why?"

"Certainly there is 'a place' in which we are promised that we shall be 'with Christ,' this world being yet the great theatre of human life and battle-ground of Satan; no place, certainly, in which to confine a happy soul without prospect of release. The Spiritualistic notion of 'circles' of dead friends revolving over us is to me intolerable. I want my husband with me when I need him, but I hope he has a place to be happy in, which is out of this woful world.

"The old astronomical idea, stars around a sun, and systems around a centre, and that centre the Throne of God, is not an unreasonable one. Isaac Taylor, among his various conjectures, inclines, I fancy, to suppose that the sun of each system is the heaven of that system. Though the glory of God may be more directly and impressively exhibited in one place than in another, we may live in different planets, and some of us, after its destruction and renovation, on this same dear old, happy and miserable, loved and maltreated earth. I hope I shall be one of them. I should like to come back and build me a beautiful home in Kansas, — I mean in what was Kansas, — among the happy people and the familiar, transfigured spots where John and I worked for God so long together. That — with my dear Lord to see and speak with every day — would be 'Heaven our Home.' "

"There will be no *days*, then?"

"There will be succession of time. There may not be alternations of twenty-four hours dark or light, but 'I use with thee an earthly language,' as the wife said in that beautiful little 'Awakening,' of Therrmin's. Do you remember it? Do read it over, if you have n't read it lately.

"As to our coming back here, there is an echo to Peter's assertion, in the idea of a world under a curse, destroyed and regenerated, — the atonement of Christ reaching, with something more than poetic force, the very sands of the earth which he trod with bleeding feet to make himself its Saviour. That makes me feel — don't you see? — what a taint there is in sin. If dumb dust is to have such awful cleansing, what must be needed for you and me?

"How many pleasant talks we have had about these things, Mary! Well, it cannot be long, at the longest, before we know, even as we are known."

I looked at her smiling white face, — it is always very white now, — and something struck slowly through me, like a chill.

October 16, midnight.

There is no such thing as sleep at present. Writing is better than thinking.

Aunt Winifred went again to Worcester to-day. She said that she had to buy trimming for Faith's sack.

She went alone, as usual, and Faith and I kept each other company through the afternoon, — she on the floor with Mary Ann, I in the easy-chair with Macaulay. As the light began to fall level on the floor, I threw the book aside, — being at the end of a volume, — and, Mary Ann having exhausted her attractions, I surrendered unconditionally to the little maiden.

She took me up garret, and down cellar, on top of the wood-pile, and into the apple-trees; I fathomed the mysteries of Old Man's Castle and Still Palm; I was her grandmother, I was her baby, I was a rabbit, I was a chestnut horse, I was a watch-dog, I was a mild-tempered giant, I was a bear, "warranted not to eat little girls," I was a roaring hippopotamus and a canary-bird, I was Jeff Davis and I was Moses in the bulrushes, and of what I was the time faileth me to tell.

It comes over me with a curious, mingled sense of the ludicrous and the horrible, that I should have spent the afternoon like a baby and almost as happily, laughing out with the child, past and future forgotten, the tremendous risks of "I spy" absorbing all my present; while what was happening was happening, and what was to come was coming. Not an echo in the air, not a prophecy in the sunshine, not a note of warning in the song of the robins that watched me from the apple-boughs!

As the long, golden afternoon slid away, we came out by the front gate to watch for the child's mother. I was tired, and, lying back on the grass, gave Faith some pink and purple larkspurs, that she might amuse herself in making a chain of them. The picture that she made sitting there on the short, dying grass — the light which broke all about her and over her at the first, creeping slowly down and away to the west, her little fingers linking the rich, bright flowers tube into tube, the dimple on her cheek and the love in her eyes — has photographed itself into my thinking.

How her voice rang out, when the wheels sounded at last, and the carriage, somewhat slowly driven, stopped! "Mamma, mamma! see what I've got for you, mamma!"

Auntie tried to step from the carriage, and called me: "Mary, can you help me a little? I am — tired."

I went to her, and she leaned heavily on my arm, and we came up the path.

"Such a pretty little chain, all for you, mamma," began Faith, and stopped, struck by her mother's look.

"It has been a long ride, and I am in pain. I believe I will lie right down on the parlor sofa. Mary, would you be kind enough to give Faith her supper and put her to bed?"

Faith's lip grieved.

"Cousin Mary is n't *you*, mamma. I want to be kissed. You have n't kissed me."

Her mother hesitated for a moment; then kissed her once, twice; put both arms about her neck; and turned her face to the wall without a word.

"Mamma is tired, dear," I said; "come away."

She was lying quite still when I had done what was to be done for the child, and had come back. The room was nearly dark. I sat down on my cricket by her sofa.

"Shall Phoebe light the lamp?"

"Not just yet."

"Can't you drink a cup of tea if I bring it?"

"Not just yet."

"Did you find the sack-trimming?" I ventured, after a pause.

I believe so, — yes." She drew a little package from her pocket, held it a moment, then let it roll to the floor forgotten. When I picked it up, the soft tissue-paper wrapper was wet and hot with tears.

"Mary?"

"Yes."

"I never thought of the little trimming till the last minute. I had another errand."

I waited.

"I thought at first I would not tell you just yet. But I suppose the time has come; it will be no more easy to put it off. I have been to Worcester all these times to see a doctor."

I bent my head in the dark, and listened for the rest.

"He has his reputation; they said he could help me if anybody could. He thought at first he could. But to-day — Mary, see here."

She walked feebly towards the window, where a faint, gray light struggled in, and opened the bosom of her dress. . . . .

There was silence between us for a long while after that; she went back to the sofa, and I took her hand and bowed my face over it, and so we sat.

The leaves rustled out of doors. Faith, up stairs, was singing herself to sleep with a droning sound.

"He talked of risking an operation," she said, at length, "but decided to-day that it was quite useless. I suppose I must give up and be sick now; I am feeling the reaction from having kept up so long. He thinks I shall not suffer a very great deal. He thinks he can relieve me, and that it may be soon over."

"There is no chance?"

"No chance."

I took both of her hands, and cried out, I believe, as I did that first night when she spoke to me of Roy, "Auntie, Auntie, Auntie!" and tried to think what I was doing, but only cried out the more.

"Why, Mary!" she said, — "why, Mary!" and again, as before, she passed her soft hand to and fro across my hair, till by and by I began to think, as I had thought before, that I could bear anything which God who loved us all — who *surely* loved us all — should send.

So then, after I had grown still, she began to tell me about it in her quiet voice, and the leaves rustled, and Faith had sung herself to sleep, and I listened wondering. For there was no pain in the quiet voice, — no pain, nor tone of fear. Indeed, it seemed to me that I detected, through its subdued sadness, a secret, suppressed buoyancy of satisfaction, with which something struggled.

"And you?" I asked, turning quickly upon her.

"I should thank God with all my heart, Mary, if it were not for Faith and you. But it *is* for Faith and you. That's all."

When I had locked the front door, and was creeping up here to my room, my foot crushed something, and a faint, wounded perfume came up. It was the little pink and purple chain.

·⊷ XVI ⊷·

"THE Lord God a'mighty help us! but His ways are past finding out. What with one thing and another thing, that child without a mother, and you with the crape not yet rusty for Mr. Roy'l, it does seem to me as if His manner of treating folks beats all! But I tell you this, Miss Mary, my dear; you jest say your prayers reg'lar and *stick to Him*, and He'll pull you through, sure!"

This was what Phoebe said when I told her.

To-night, for the first time, Auntie fairly gave up trying to put Faith to bed. She had insisted on it until now, crawling up by the banisters like a wounded thing. This time she tottered and sank upon the second step. She cried out, feebly: "I am afraid I must give it up to Cousin Mary. Faith!" — the child clung with both hands to her — "Faith, Faith! Mother's little girl?"

It was the last dear care of motherhood yielded; the last link snapped. It seemed to be the very bitterness of parting.

I turned away, that they might bear it together, they two alone.

19th.

Yet I think that took away the sting.

The days are slipping away now very quietly, and — to her I am sure, and to me for her sake — very happily.

She suffers less than I had feared, and she lies upon the bed and smiles, and Faith comes in and plays about, and the cheery morning sunshine falls on everything, and when her strong hours come, we have long talks together, hand clasped in hand.

Such pleasant talks! We are quite brave to speak of anything, since we know that what is to be is best just so, and since we fear no parting. I tell her that Faith and I will soon learn to shut our eyes and think we see her, and try to make it *almost* the same, for she will never be very far away, will she? And then she shakes her head smiling, for it pleases her, and she kisses me softly. Then we dream of how it will all be, and how we shall love and try to please each other quite as much as now.

"It will be like going around a corner, don't you see?" she says. "You will know that I am there all the while, though hidden, and that if you call me I shall hear." Then we talk of Faith, and of how I shall comfort her; that I shall teach her this, and guard her from that, and how I shall talk with her about heaven and her mother. Sometimes Faith comes up and wants to know what we are saying, and lays poor Mary Ann, sawdust and all, upon the pillow, and wants "her toof-ache kissed away." So Auntie kisses away the dolly's "toof-ache"; and kisses the dolly's little mother, sometimes with a quiver on her lips, but more often with a smile in her eyes, and Faith runs back to play, and her laugh ripples out, and her mother listens — listens —

Sometimes, too, we talk of some of the people for whom she cares; of her husband's friends; of her scholars, or Dr. Bland, or Clo, or poor 'Bin Quirk, or of somebody down town whom she was planning to help this winter. Little Clo comes in as often as she is strong enough to see her, and sends

over untold jellies and blanc-manges, which Faith and I have
to eat. "But don't let the child know that," Auntie says.

But more often we talk of the life which she is so soon to
begin; of her husband and Roy; of what she will try to say
to Christ; how much dearer He has grown to her since she
has lain here in pain at His bidding, and how He helps her, at
morning and at eventide and in the night-watches.

We talk of the trees and the mountains and the lilies in the
garden, on which the glory of the light that is not the light of
the sun may shine; of the "little brooks" by which she longs to
sit and sing to Faith; of the treasures of art which she may
fancy to have about her; of the home in which her husband
may be making ready for her coming, and wonder what he
has there, and if he knows how near the time is now.

But I notice lately that she more often and more quickly
wearies of these things; that she comes back, and comes back
again to some loving thought — as loving as a child's — of
Jesus Christ. He seems to be — as she once said she tried that
He should be to Faith — her *"best* friend."

Sometimes, too, we wonder what it means to pass out of
the body, and what one will be first conscious of.

"I used to have a very human, and by no means slight, dread
of the physical pain of death," she said to-day; "but, for some
reason or other, that is slowly leaving me. I imagine that the
suffering of any fatal sickness is worse than the immediate
process of dissolution. Then there is so much beyond it to
occupy one's thoughts. One thing I have thought much about;
it is that, whatever may be our first experience after leaving
the body, it is not likely to be a *revolutionary* one. It is more
in analogy with God's dealings that a quiet process, a gentle
accustoming, should open our eyes on the light that would
blind if it came in a flash. Perhaps we shall not see Him, —
perhaps we could not bear it to see Him at once. It may be
that the faces of familiar human friends will be the first to

greet us; it may be that the touch of the human hand dearer than any but His own shall lead us, as we are able, behind the veil, till we are a little used to the glory and the wonder, and lead us so to Him.

"Be that as it may, and be heaven where it may, I am not afraid. With all my guessing and my studying and my dreaming over these things, I am only a child in the dark. 'Nevertheless, I am not afraid of the dark.' God bless Mr. Robertson for saying that! I'm going to bless him when I see him. How pleasant it will be to see him, and some other friends whose faces I never saw in this world! David, for instance, or Paul, or Cowper, or President Lincoln, or Mrs. Browning. The only trouble is that *I* am nobody to them! However, I fancy that they will let me shake hands with them.

"No, I am quite willing to trust all these things to God.

> 'And what if much be still unknown?
> Thy Lord shall teach thee that,
> When thou shalt stand before His throne,
> Or sit as Mary sat.'

I may find them very different from what I have supposed. I know that I shall find them infinitely *more* satisfying than I have supposed. As Schiller said of his philosophy, 'Perhaps I may be ashamed of my raw design, at sight of the true original. This may happen; I expect it; but then, if reality bears no resemblance to my dreams, it will be a more majestic, a more delightful surprise.'

"I believe nothing that God denies. I cannot overrate the beauty of his promise. So it surely can have done no harm for me to take the comfort of my fancying till I am there; and what a comfort it has been to me, God only knows. I could scarcely have borne some things without it."

"You are never afraid that anything proving a little different from what you expect might —"

"Might disappoint me? No; I have settled that in my heart with God. I do not *think* I shall be disappointed. The truth is, he has obviously not *opened* the gates which bar heaven from our sight, but he has as obviously not *shut* them; they stand ajar, with the Bible and reason in the way, to keep them from closing; surely we should look in as far as we can, and surely, if we look with reverence, our eyes will be holden, that we may not cheat ourselves with mirages. And, as the little Swedish girl said, the first time she saw the stars: 'O father, if the *wrong side* of heaven is so beautiful, what must the *right side* be?' "

January.

I write little now, for I am living too much. The days are stealing away and lessening one by one, and still Faith plays about the room, though very softly now, and still the cheery sunshine shimmers in, and still we talk with clasping hands, less often and more pleasantly. Morning and noon and evening come and go; the snow drifts down and the rain falls softly; clouds form and break and hurry past the windows; shadows melt and lights are shattered, and little rainbows are prisoned by the icicles that hang from the eaves.

I sit and watch them, and watch the sick-lamp flicker in the night, and watch the blue morning crawl over the hills; and the old words are stealing down my thought: *That is the substance, this the shadow; that the reality, this the dream.*

I watch her face upon the pillow; the happy secret on its lips; the smile within its eyes. It is nearly a year now since God sent the face to me. What it has done for me He knows; what the next year and all the years are to be without it. He knows, too.

It is slipping away, — slipping. And I — must — lose it.

Perhaps I should not have said what I said to-night; but being weak from watching, and seeing how glad she was to go, seeing how all the peace was for her, all the pain for us, I cried, "O Auntie, Auntie, why can't we go too? Why *can't* Faith and I go with you?"

But she answered me only, "Mary, He knows."

We will be brave again to-morrow. A little more sunshine in the room! A little more of Faith and the dolly!

The Sabbath.

She asked for the child at bedtime to-night, and I laid her down in her night-dress on her mother's arm. She kissed her, and said her prayers, and talked a bit about Mary Ann, and to-morrow, and her snow man. I sat over by the window in the dusk, and watched a little creamy cloud that was folding in the moon. Presently their voices grew low, and at last Faith's stopped altogether. Then I heard in fragments this: —

"Sleepy, dear? But you won't have many more talks with mamma. Keep awake just a minute, Faith, and hear — can you hear? Mamma will never, *never* forget her little girl; she won't go away very far; she will always love you. Will you remember as long as you live? She will always see you, though you can't see her, perhaps. Hush, my darling, *don't* cry! Is n't God naughty? No, God is good; God is always good. He won't take mamma a great way off. One more kiss? There! now you may go to sleep. One more! Come, Cousin Mary."

June 6.

It is a long time since I have written here. I did not want to open the book till I was sure that I could open it quietly, and could speak as she would like to have me speak, of what remains to be written.

But a very few words will tell it all.

It happened so naturally and so happily, she was so glad when the time came, and she made me so glad for her sake, that I cannot grieve. I say it from my honest heart, I cannot grieve. In the place out of which she has gone, she has left me peace. I think of something that Miss Procter said about the opening of that golden gate,[18]

> "round which the kneeling spirits wait.
> The halo seems to linger round those kneeling closest to the door:
> The joy that lightened from that place shines still upon the watcher's
>   face."

I think more often of some things that she herself said in the very last of those pleasant talks, when, turning a leaf in her little Bible, she pointed out to me the words: —

"It is expedient for you that I go away; for, if I go not away, the Comforter will not come."

It was one spring-like night, — the twenty-ninth of March.

She had been in less pain, and had chatted and laughed more with us than for many a day. She begged that Faith might stay till dark, and might bring her Noah's ark and play down upon the foot of the bed where she could see her. I sat in the rocking-chair with my face to the window. We did not light the lamps.

The night came on slowly. Showery clouds flitted by, but there was a blaze of golden color behind them. It broke through and scattered them; it burned them and melted them; it shot great pink and purple jets up to the zenith; it fell and lay in amber mist upon the hills. A soft wind swept by, and darted now and then into the glow, and shifted it about, color away from color, and back again.

"See, Faith!" she said softly; "put down the little camel a minute, and look!" and added after, but neither to the child nor to me, it seemed: "At eventide there shall be light." Phoebe knocked presently, and I went out to see what was wanted, and planned a little for Auntie's breakfast, and came back.

[18] Adelaide Procter (1825–1864), the daughter of "Barry Cornwall," was the author of *Legends and Lyrics* (1858). She is remembered today for the poem "The Lost Chord."

Faith, with her little ark, was still playing quietly upon the bed. I sat down again in my rocking-chair with my face to the window. Now and then the child's voice broke the silence, asking Where should she put the elephant, and was there room there for the yellow bird? and now and then her mother answered her, and so presently the skies had faded, and so the night came on.

I was thinking that it was Faith's bedtime, and that I had better light the lamp, when a few distinct, hurried words from the bed attracted my attention.

"Faith, I think you had better kiss mamma now, and get down."

There was a change in the voice. I was there in a moment, and lifted the child from the pillow, where she had crept. But she said, "Wait a minute, Mary; wait a minute," — for Faith clung to her, with one hand upon her cheek, softly patting it.

I went over and stood by the window.

It was her mother herself who gently put the little fingers away at last. "Mother's own little girl! Good night, my darling, my darling."

So I took the child away to Phoebe, and came back, and shut the door.

"I thought you might have some message for Roy," she said.

"Now?"

"Now, I think."

We had often talked of this, and she had promised to remember it, whatever it might be. So I told her — But I will not write what I told her.

I saw that she was playing weakly with her wedding-ring, which hung very loosely below its little worn guard.

"Take the little guard," she said, "and keep it for Faith; but bury the other with me: he put it on: nobody else must take it — "

The sentence dropped, unfinished.

I crept up on the bed beside her, for she seemed to wish it. I asked if I should light the lamp, but she shook her head. The room seemed light, she said, quite light. She wondered then if Faith were asleep, and if she would waken early in the morning.

After that I kissed her, and then we said nothing more, only presently she asked me to hold her hand.

It was quite dark when she turned her face at last towards the window.

"John!" she said, — "why, John!"

*   *   *   *   *   *   *

They came in, with heads uncovered and voices hushed, to see her, in the days while she was lying down stairs among the flowers.

Once when I thought that she was alone, I went in, — it was at twilight, — and turned, startled by a figure that was crouched sobbing on the floor.

"O, I want to go too, *I want* to go too!" it cried.

"She's ben there all day long," said Phoebe, wiping her eyes, "and she won't go home for a mouthful of victuals, poor creetur! but she jest sets there and cries and cries, an' there's no stoppin' of her!"

It was little Clo.

At another time, I was there with fresh flowers, when the door opened, creaking a little, and 'Bin Quirk came in on tiptoe, trying in vain to still the noise of his new boots. His eyes were red and wet, and he held out to me timidly a single white carnation.

"Could you put it somewhere, where it would n't do any harm? I walked way over to Worcester and back to get it. If you could jest hide it under the others out of sight, seems to me it would do me a sight of good to feel it was there, you know."

I motioned to him to lay it himself between her fingers.

"O, I dars n't. I'm not fit, *I'm* not. She'd rether have you."

But I told him that I knew she would be as pleased that he should give it to her himself as she was when he gave her the China pinks on that distant summer day. So the great awkward fellow bent down, as simply as a child, as tenderly as a woman, and left the flower in its place.

"*She* liked 'em," he faltered; "maybe, if what she used to say is all so, she'll like 'em now. She liked 'em better than she did machines. I've just got my carpet-sweeper through; I was thinking how pleased she'd be; I wanted to tell her. If I should go to the good place, — if ever I do go, it will be just her doin's, — I'll tell her then, maybe, I — "

He forgot that anybody was there, and, sobbing, hid his face in his great hands.

So we are waiting for the morning when the gates shall open, — Faith and I. I, from my stiller watches, am not saddened by the music of her life. I feel sure that her mother wishes it to be a cheery life. I feel sure that she is showing me, who will have no motherhood by which to show myself, how to help her little girl.

And Roy, — ah, well, and Roy, — he knows. Our hour is not yet come. If the Master will that we should be about His Father's business, what is that to us?

THE JOHN HARVARD LIBRARY

The intent of
Waldron Phoenix Belknap, Jr.,
as expressed in an early will, was for
Harvard College to use the income from a
permanent trust fund he set up, for "editing and
publishing rare, inaccessible, or hitherto unpublished
source material of interest in connection with the
history, literature, art (including minor and useful
art), commerce, customs, and manners or way of
life of the Colonial and Federal Periods of the United
States . . . In all cases the emphasis shall be on the
presentation of the basic material." A later testament
broadened this statement, but Mr. Belknap's inter-
ests remained constant until his death.

In linking the name of the first benefactor of
Harvard College with the purpose of this later,
generous-minded believer in American culture the
John Harvard Library seeks to emphasize the impor-
tance of Mr. Belknap's purpose. The John Harvard
Library of the Belknap Press of Harvard University
Press exists to make books and documents
about the American past more readily
available to scholars and the
general reader.